Slobbers & Sleuths

WRITTEN & ILLUSTRATED BY
MARI MEEHAN

This book is a work of fiction. The characters, places and events in this story are fictional. Any similarities to real people, places, or events are not intentional and purely the result of coincidence.

Formatting by Self-Publishing Services, LLC

Published by Yellow Snow Publishing

Hardcover ISBN: 978-1-63649-670-2
Paperback ISBN: 978-1-63649-671-9

Library of Congress Control Number: 2020918290

Dedicated to all those who have helped bring Slobbers to life and are helping him live it!

SLOBBERS

"No! Noooo. He's dead!" Bud's voice is quivering. He's staring wide-eyed at the big man standing beside him. "Cole Black is supposed to be dead!"

All of our emotions are crackling like the fire in front of us. What just happened? This man I've lived with since growing too big to live with Bud's family has just revealed he's the "lost boy,"

Cole Black, who disappeared from the Village of Serenity years ago.

People think he is dead because no sign of him has ever been found. Or so we all thought. But here he is. Very much alive.

Cole furrows his brow and stares at Bud long and hard. Bud takes a step backward. Bro and I shift ourselves from lethargic watching to full alert.

"He is... ***I*** am not dead. You can see I'm not." His voice is low and very quiet. "The story you've heard is no more true than the ones that say I took growth hormones so I could play football."

"But...but why?" Bud looks confused, his mouth drooping at the corners.

Bro and I are confused, too. I call him Bro 'cause he's my twin brother, but other than the four of us together now, everyone thinks he's me—Slobbers—and calls him that. Ya see, we swapped places when I got too big to live with Bud and the rest of my family, and he was livin' with Cole. Bro just didn't get into to that growth stuff that made me, the snails, and Cole turn into giants. Man, you talk about confusing. I guess this is why what happened to Cole is a big mystery.

"Why...why didn't you tell me? I thought you trusted me," Bud stammers. "Why didn't you at least tell your parents? How could you let them think you're dead?"

"You have no idea what the real story is." Cole's voice is still very quiet, but it has a bit of an edge to it. He pulls up his collar and pokes at the dwindling fire with a stick. "I hope you'll give me a chance to explain before you go jumping to any more conclusions."

"Explain? You've never explained anything to me. Like why you live like...like this! Like a hermit." Bud waves his arm at the fire and the woods around us. "How can you be so good and kind and smart and yet be..."

"And yet be what?"

"I dunno. So secretive."

"Secretive? You've never asked me anything. Ever. And I'm not as secretive as you seem to think." Cole studies Bud, then shrugs his shoulders. His voice returns to normal.

Whew. This is a relief. That really low, quiet voice was kinda unsettling.

"I'll tell you this. The story that circulates around Serenity is not the truth. It's complicated. I'll tell you all of it, and I'll even show you proof that the stories you've heard aren't true."

"I've always looked up to you, you know? I want to know the truth. I really do!"

"I know Bud, and I've always been honest with you. That won't change. I never said anything because it's all pretty hard to understand."

"Why? Because I'm just a kid?" Bud asks. "I'm just so...so confused. You've been such a great friend..."

"I'm still your friend. I will always be your friend. Slobbers and Little Slobbers here are our bond. It can't and won't be broken. And it's not just because you're a kid. It's because it's...complicated." He pauses for a minute then suddenly blurts out, "Now scoot. Before your mother starts to worry. Come back when you have time, and we'll have a good talk. I promise. Can I trust you to keep everything quiet until then?"

Their eyes are glued to one another. "I...I've always kept my word to you...Cole."

Cole nods. Bro goes to Bud's side. He and I exchange glances, wondering what will happen now. They turn away and head toward the meadow.

Cole lets out a long sigh as they disappear out of sight. We go into our cave, where he slumps into his chair. He wipes his face with his hand and stares into the fire. *Awooooo.* I nuzzle his hand, hoping to reassure him it's gonna be okay. I know Bud well, and he isn't one to go against his word. He's really a good kid. I think he just wants to know the story. *Heck, so do I.* I wonder how much Bro knows. Probably a lot more than I do because he lived with Cole before we switched places.

After a few minutes, Cole gets up from his chair and begins rummaging through a stack of his book boxes. He's really restless. I've never seen him like this. It must be some story! He unearths

a box from the bottom of a stack and shuffles through the books. He pulls one out and lays it on the floor in front of me.

"It's all in here, Slobbers, every untrue word about what everyone believes happened. False assumptions and outright lies. So long ago," he mutters. "So long ago. What am I supposed to do?"

He plops down on the floor looking glum. I nose the book and look carefully at the pictures. I can't read, but I learn a lot from pictures. Something slips out from between the pages. Cole picks up a couple of scraps of cloth.

"Just remembrances," he mutters again. "Bitter remembrances. I just can't let it...them go."

I sniff each piece thoroughly, being careful not to slobber on them. They sure have distinct odors. Odors I'll have no trouble remembering.

Cole puts the scraps back in the book and sets it on the table. "I'll be wanting to show all this to Bud," he says. "I sure hope I'm not making a mistake."

You're not. You're not.

I'm hoping he won't blow the opportunity to get whatever this is all about off his chest. Like, as Bud asked, why *is* he livin' like this? I mean, like how many people live in a cave?

I never really thought about it before, but boy, I'm thinkin' about it now.

BRO

Bud shuffles along, kicking at the fallen leaves that crunch under our feet. He doesn't even want to play fetch with me like we usually do on these walks home. It's like I'm not even here.

And it's so unlike him. He's usually so cheerful.

Roooff! I gallop around him a bit, but he's ignoring me. *Okay*. He's really upset with Cole. Cole. None of us knew his name! Why didn't someone, like Bud who can talk, ask before now?

People are pretty obvious when they want us dogs to do something like come or sit or lay down, so we don't pay much attention to names, but people use them all the time. I guess Bud just didn't think about asking.

~

Instead of doing his homework, after dinner Bud just sits on the edge of his bed, his eyes fixed on the floor. I ache for him. I know what it's like to not understand things and have no one to explain them. Like what happened to Slobbers when we got separated at the shelter last spring when we were just babies. It's the loneliest feeling in the world. Bud slides from the bed to the floor and pulls me onto his lap. I lick his cheek. *Hmmm. Salty. Is that a tear?* He really *is* upset.

~

The next day brings no change. I'm hoping he won't tell anyone what's bothering him until Cole has the chance to explain things to him.

And to Slobbers and me, for that matter! Cole never talked about his past when I lived with him. I gotta admit, though, livin' in a cave *is* pretty weird.

After dinner, the doorbell rings. I squeeze past Dad's and Mom's legs and greet—Deon's dad! He's really a neat guy. He owns the local newspaper and says he's wondering if Bud would like a delivery route because his son Deon, Bud's best friend, has one.

"Let's ask him," Dad says.

We settle in the family room.

"Bud?" Dad goes to the stairs and calls, "C'mon down here. You've got company."

He comes skulking into the room, shuffling his feet, but he perks up when he sees Mr. Brown. "Mr. Brown? Hi."

His mood really brightens as Mr. Brown explains the job, how much money Bud will earn, and that I will be Bud's helper.

Wow! This is pretty cool! Me, Super Saint the delivery dog! Slobbers has nothin' on me! Yeah, well, actually he does. For now, anyway.

"You and Deon can meet and come to the village together to pick up your papers. That way you'll be safe until you get to the areas that are well-lighted. When you're both done, you can meet again to come back home."

"Super! I'll do a really great job for you, Mr. Brown. I promise!"

The excitement in his voice makes me happy. Maybe it will take his mind off the mystery of Cole Black for a while.

Sis comes bounding into the room, whining, "Why can't I have a paper route?"

I roll my eyes and prepare for the drama. She is soooo good at drama.

"I'd like to earn some money, too!"

Oops.

"Well, Sis," Mr. Brown says, "This is a fairly long route, and the papers are heavy."

"Slobbers can help me just as well as he can help Bud. He'll figure out a way to make Slobbers carry them anyway. I know Bud!"

"You do not!" Now they're both whining.

Arrrroooo. I add my own whine. Enough already!

"Quiet, both of you, or neither one of you will get the job!" Mom says sternly. "Where are your manners?"

They're both sulking, shuffling their feet and staring at the floor.

"How 'bout this?" Mr. Brown suggests, winking at Dad and Mom. "Since there are no more current openings, how 'bout you can substitute when either Bud or Deon have a school conflict or catch a cold or something like that? You'll have to have someone with you, though. Slobbers is great, but I'd feel better if there were two of you. Maybe Lin's folks would allow her to go with you. I am just leery about having you kids out in the early morning hours alone."

"We'll have Slobbers," Sis assures him.

"Having Slobbers with you, either of you, is a must," Mr. Brown says firmly. "So, Sis, what do you think?"

"I'll ask Lin," she mutters. Lin is her best friend. "I guess it's better than nuthin'."

"Good girl. When you know her answer, let me know so I can put the two of you on the substitute list."

After Mr. Brown leaves, Dad and Mom give Bud and Sis a good scolding for being so rude. They're both sulking as they go off to their rooms. *Wow. Is this an awkward age for kids or what?* I'm sure glad tonight's my night to sleep with Mom and Dad! *Sheesh.*

SLOBBERS

The days are getting shorter and the temperatures cooler. I kinda like it now that my coat is heavy and thick. This being my first year on this place called Earth, I'm sure having a lot of interesting experiences.

Besides changes in my coat and going from adorable to gangly, there are other things, too.

For instance, every morning, Cole and I head out on one of the paths that lead to and from our cave. Boy, I'm learning a lot on these trips because he talks to me nonstop. I nose around everything, finding holes in the ground and under logs and in trees, and Cole tells me what kind of animal lives in them. Let's see, squirrels live in holes in trees. Chipmunks are everywhere. Groundhogs live in holes in the ground. That figures. "Ground." I get that, but they don't look at all like hogs. So why are they called groundhogs?

Beavers live in stick houses that they build themselves from trees they chew down, and that are mostly underwater. Wow, how do they breathe? This is so cool! Sometimes we even see them.

Others, Cole tells me, come out only at night. Like skunks and raccoons and possums and owls. He tells me if I get too close to a skunk, I'm gonna smell worse than the snails I hate so much. Whew! If it smells like rotten eggs, it's a skunk! I sure don't wanna get that stuff in my fur! To get it out, Cole says he'd have to give me a bath in tomato juice.

Ugh. Who wants to a get a bath in that stuff? It's sticky and icky and doesn't smell all that good, either. Where would he get tomato juice anyway?

He shows me what other animals' poop looks like. Each is different. Some are similar to my own. Others are pellets. Some big, some tiny. Owls are really different. They have huge pellets that are full of teeny-weeny bones and leftover fur or feathers from their dinners.

He shows me shredded bark on tree trunks and low-hanging limbs where deer rub a soft covering called velvet off their antlers. I thought velvet was like for pillows and stuff. I'm learning that people language is strange. One word can have a lot of different meanings, and we're supposed to know what they're talkin' about! He talks about different birds and where they nest and which ones stick around in the winter.

He even shows me moss he's saved up, so if he comes across an injured animal, he can put it on a wound and the stuff in it will keep the wound from getting infected. The moss can even help ease pain.

Wow. He sure knows a lot. I've never seen anything like this on television. I guess he learns it from all his books. It's really neat, though, and now that some smaller animals are getting used to my being around, sometimes they come out to see us. Like chipmunks and even the squirrels I still love to chase, even though it's harder in the woods. I still pounce at them, though, just for fun. They just chatter, teasing me, and go about their business gathering nuts and seeds and stuff. I've even seen foxes and, of course, deer.

Some other guys I haven't seen, yet. Big guys like bears and moose and wolves. And cougars and bobcats. Cole tells me not to try to play with any of them because they aren't playful types, except with their own kind. They live higher up in the mountains, he tells me. The bears even find their own caves for the winter and stay in them until spring. They sleep! I like to sleep, too, but

there's a limit. *Don't they get hungry? How long is winter anyway?*

The longer I live with Cole, the more I like him. He cares so much about everything that's around us. It makes me feel sad that something has driven him from his home and family, but the animals here in the woods are sure lucky to have him as a friend.

We walk farther and farther now to places I didn't know existed. Like the ski resort. Skis, he explains, are long, board-type things people attach to their feet so they can slide down mountains. Humans do the strangest things. Sometimes there are huge snowslides called avalanches, he tells me. He worries about one place in particular that's on our side of the ski resort and isn't far from our cave. We pass that one particular area a lot. It's a cross-country course where, instead of skiing down a mountain, people just glide along on flat surfaces. It's near one of those snowslide areas, and he worries someone could get caught in one.

Of course, first it will have to snow, but he assures me it's not far off. He says he can tell by the feel of the air, and, sometimes, he can smell it. *Oh ho! Maybe he has a little Saint Bernard in him! Nah. His nose is nowhere near as big as mine.* That's why we can smell all kinds of things. I can't wait to find out what snow smells like.

We have all the time we want, and we just wander and wander. Sometimes we don't even go back to the cave at night. Cole will make a bed for each of us out of pine branches, and, in some places, there are even shelters he's made in case the weather gets really bad. With a nice crackling fire and some good stuff to eat from the bag he carries, it's not a bad way to spend a night every now and then. We don't do it often. Not unless something he sees or hears bothers him.

I'm always happy to get back to our cave. The crackling fires in the woods are nice, but I like the fire he builds in our fireplace the most. It's bigger, and I can just lie in front of it and watch the flames dance. Or snooze while Cole reads or whittles. He does a lot of that, too, making neat stuff out of sticks. He even made one that looks like a wee, little me. It's home, and I'm happy.

BRO

Whew, this paper route business is a lotta work. Especially so early in the morning. It's not like my usual walks where I can just loaf along and sniff all the new smells and a bunch of old ones. It's strictly business. Mom sewed two bags together so they sling across my back. I carry all the papers for Bud. I don't really mind. They're not all that heavy for a big, strong Saint Bernard like me.

Bud takes them right up to people's doors. His customers seem to appreciate it because even the first time he collected money from them, they all gave him something extra. He calls them tips. He always gave them a big, "Thank you very much!" I guess the papers aren't free. The people who write the stories have to get paid and, of course, Mr. Brown and Deon and Bud.

~

Bud and I have only been on our new job a few weeks when, at dinner, he looks kind of down.

"Is something wrong, Bud?" Mom asks.

"Kind of," Bud is looking at Sis out of the corner of his eye. "I think I might need Sis to help with the papers for a while."

Sis looks up beaming. "Really? For how long? Are you gonna pay me?"

"Of course," Bud says with a groan.

"What's up?" Dad asks.

"Well, the robotics club is going to enter a competition, and, to get ready, we're gonna have to work before school for maybe a couple of weeks. Too many of the kids already have stuff going on after school. I don't see how I can do both the papers and the club. The papers aren't ready early enough for me to go any earlier than I do now. And I really want to take part in the competition."

"I can do it! I can do it!" Sis chirps happily. "Mr. and Mrs. Huang said Lin can help, and I promised I'd split what I earn with her."

"Sis can come with me this weekend, and Lin, too, if she wants, to see how the job is to be done,"

Bud says. "But you don't get paid until you're doin' it for real. And I do the route on weekends."

"Oooo." Sis sulks.

"Sheesh, do you wanna do it or not?" Bud gripes. "You can start for real Monday if you want. Or else I'll have Mr. Brown find another sub."

"I think you can live with that, Sis," Dad says, laughing and winking at Mom. "After all, Bud will be doing double duty, his job and showing you and Lin the ropes."

This should be interesting. When Sis and Lin are together, they're all giggles. I'm wondering how much patience Bud is going to have when he's trying to teach them.

Saturday morning way before dawn, we meet Deon and Lin and head to the village. The papers are ready for us at the newspaper office.

"Good luck," Deon grins, playfully punching Bud's arm before he heads off in another direction.

"Yeah," Bud mutters. He mutters a lot lately.

We walk briskly to the beginning of Bud's route. "Now cut the giggles," he hisses. "People are still asleep. Especially on weekends. Now pay attention. This is important." He folds a paper. The girls watch intently. He walks to the first door and places it under a mat if there is one or puts a stone on it if there isn't.

The girls nod then take off like they've been doing it forever. I bet they've been practicing just in case they got their chance.

"How'd they do?" Deon asks as we all meet behind the pub to head home.

"Okay for beginners," Bud says.

The girls giggle.

~

I sleep in Sis's room Sunday night to make sure she gets up bright and early Monday. I'm nudging her with my nose as she tries to push me away when Bud knocks loudly. "Rise and shine, Sis. We gotta get going."

The two gigglers really surprise me. They giggle with each other all the way to the newspaper office but say very little as we go about our work. Lin folds the papers, and Sis takes them to the doors. As soon as we finish, they start giggling. They giggle even more as we meet Deon.

Girls. I don't know. Girl dogs don't act this way. Why do human girls?

There's so much about humans I don't understand, and it seems to get more confusing the more I'm around them. I really don't understand all the giggling. At least it's not as bad as when they're in their drama mode.

~

After we finish our route, the girls and I wait for Deon behind the pub. The shadows from the stored barrels are eerie. Deon approaches silently and startles us.

"What?" he says.

"Shhh," Lin says. "Something caught my eye. It looked like someone was moving around in the shadows behind the pub."

"Probably someone coming to work," Deon hisses. "Let's get going. I want my breakfast before I have to leave for school!"

~

I'm lying in the family room as Sis and Lin come running in after school.

"I still think I saw someone," Lin is saying.

"It was probably one of the workmen, like Deon said," Sis tells her.

"Yeah, probably. But I'm not so sure."

Bud comes in and drops his backpack with a thud. Lin pounces as he heads for the fridge. "Have you ever seen anyone behind the pub early in the morning?" she asks.

"Not really," he tells her. "Why?"

"I think I saw someone yesterday. Deon thought it might be someone coming to work, but it's awfully early."

"It could have been the shadows playing tricks on your eyes if it wasn't someone coming to work. What with your imagination and all."

"Yeah," Sis says, "or it could have been someone up to no good."

Bud rolls his eyes. "Look, keep an eye out for the next few mornings and see if you see anything again. Then we'll deal with it."

"Okay," Lin agrees enthusiastically.

SLOBBERS

The familiar crunching of leaves announces the approach of visitors. It can only be Bud and Bro. *Oh boy, oh boy! It's been awhile!*

Cole hears them too. "C'mon Slobbers, let's go meet them." We wait in our usual place as they make their way through the now leafless trees.

Woof, woof! Bro and I greet each other by batting paws and bumping noses and rolling in the leaves.

"Hello, Bud," Cole says. "I was beginning to think you weren't coming back."

"Hi," Bud returns the greeting. "Been a lot going on at school, plus I have a paper route now." He goes on quickly. "I haven't been able to stop thinking about you, who you are, and that you're alive." Bud looks up at his friend. "Then I get to thinkin' about all sorts of stuff, and I don't understand anything."

"Let's go get warm. I want to show you where I live. It's a cave. Actually, a pretty nice cave."

It is really nice, it is, and I want to tell Bud. Rrrooof.

"A cave? A cave? Are you kidding me? Why are you living in a cave?"

Bud's eyes widen as it comes into sight. "Wow! You actually live here?"

"I do, and it's really not so bad. It stays cool in the summer, and the fireplace keeps it nice and snug in the winter. We have plenty of water from the stream. It usually doesn't freeze because it runs so fast, but we can melt snow if we need to. We have light at night from the fire and from oil lamps, and we have plenty of food that we cook over the fire when it's too cold or windy to cook outside."

Bud is looking around in wonder. Bro and I romp a bit more but are keeping a close eye on them.

"Why didn't you build yourself a cabin?" Bud asks as he looks around. "This really *is* neat though. How'd ya fix it up so nice?"

"To answer your first question, a cabin would be too easy to find. To your second question, with a lot of patience over a lot of time," Cole says. "Grab a seat."

Cole motions to his easy chair as he pulls up the chair from his table for himself.

"Whatcha building outside?" Bud asks referring to the shelter Cole is working on under an outcropping of rock next to our entrance.

"I'm doing some repair work on the place I bring animals. Getting it ready for winter. Sometimes they get hurt and need a safe place to heal up, and I try to keep them as warm and as comfortable and as safe as I can."

"That's pretty cool. Does it happen often?"

"Not too often, but I like to be ready just in case. I think we may have a bad winter this year, which increases the risk. I just sort of feel it."

"Is it because you live out here where you're really right in nature and everything?"

"Yeah, maybe. I've learned to sense a lot of things, like changes in the weather, from what I see and feel and sometimes even smell."

"Man, this is awesome!" Bud is looking around the cave. "You read a lot?" He nods toward the boxes of books.

"Not much else to do during long winter evenings," Cole laughs. "They pass pretty fast, though, with a good book."

"No computer, huh? Of course not. No electricity. Man, I've never imagined anything like this even existed. Are there more caves around here and more men like you? The villagers talk about caves and monsters being out here in the woods."

"Well, I've been here for a good many years, and I've never come across another cave this large nor another human being living anywhere near."

"How'd you find it?"

Cole sighs. "Well, when I left home and was just wandering aimlessly, I happened across it. It provided me with much-needed shelter, and everything else just sort of happened."

"Just sort of happened? How could all this just sorta happen?"

Cole leans back on his chair and crosses his hands behind his head. "Looking back, with the knowledge I have now, I might have done things differently," he says, "but I was just a boy, not much older than you. I was scared. No one believed what I tried to tell them. Even my friends turned against me. My father disowned me. He said I was no son of his. That hurt me so much. I figured if I wasn't wanted, I'd just disappear. I had hunted enough and camped enough that I knew how to survive, if only barely. I knew the woods pretty well because I played here a lot, and I knew how to keep an eye out for people looking for me. After a time, they stopped. So, I just kept on with the life I had made for myself. That's how it just sort of happened."

Bro and I are curled against each other, fascinated.

"Everyone thinks you're dead though!"

"I've thought about it for a very long time. It's better this way."

"I know you're alive, and I'm darn glad!"

Cole smiles. "I'm glad you're glad."

"I don't get it," Bud says. "That was so long ago. Don't you think people would at least like to know you're alive? And okay?"

"I don't know." Cole looks at his feet. "I don't know if things can change. It's been this way for so long."

"Where do you get stuff like your books...and this chair...and stuff?"

"You'd be surprised how wasteful people can be," Cole says. "With patience and knowing where to look, it's amazing what can be found."

Bud nods. "I guess that could happen."

"Hey, would you like a cup of really good tea? It's my own brew." Cole walks to what is our kitchen, fills a pot with water and hangs it on a hook over the fire.

"Sure. Can I look around while it's brewing?"

"Help yourself."

I nod to Bro to stay put while I get up and move to Bud's side, easing him over to where the scrapbook with the clippings about Cole's disap-

pearance still lays open. He notices it as I hoped he would and begins reading.

"Wow, you really did make headlines, didn't you?" As he turns a page, a couple of pieces of cloth fall to the floor. "What are these?" he asks.

Cole glances at Bud. "Some bad memories," he says. "Here," he offers Bud a mug of steaming hot tea. "What do you think?"

Bud takes a deep whiff then a tentative sip. "Ohhhh, this is good!" He grins and takes another sip. "Cole...can...can I ask you something? I don't want you to get mad or anything."

Cole's eyebrow arches.

"I'd...I'd like you to meet my dad. Things are so different today than they used to be, and maybe he could help. He's really great and would keep your secret if you really want him to. I know he'd like you, and I think you'd like him, too."

Cole studies Bud closely. "I think I'd like your dad, too." He smiles. "After all, he is your dad. I...just don't want to stir things up again. As long as it's been, you know, I still smart from it, and then there is my size. Look at my hands. They're as big as bear paws, and I have to make my own moccasins 'cause discarded shoes I've found don't come close to fitting. I couldn't walk through a door standing up if my life depended on it. I...I'm a...a freak!"

"Not to me! Neither is Slobbers. Look, after the snail stuff was over, Dad told me I could talk to him about anything. Because I didn't when I knew the guy at the health club was probably dealing the stuff that was making the snails and even Slobbers grow. We didn't tell anybody, and look what happened! I know you can trust him."

Cole seems to be weighing the idea. *Boy, oh boy, would that be great! Dad would know exactly what to do. He's a really smart guy.*

"Please?" Bud pleaded.

"I know you mean well Bud; I...I'm just not sure I'm ready. Making myself known to you was a huge step for me. If it hadn't been for our pair of Slobberses, I probably wouldn't have done it."

"Would you at least think about it? Please?" Bud asked.

Cole smiled at his young friend, taking the now empty mug. "I'll think about it," he said softly. "I'll think about it."

Bud pumped his fist. "Yes!"

Bro and I bark with joy as we thump the ground with our tails. *Woof, woof, woof, woof!*

BRO

I really like it now that the weather is getting cooler. I don't think the girls like it quite as much. There's a lot of foot stomping and blowing on cold fingers. Their spirits are high, though, because they're earning some money. I wonder what they'll do with it after they get it. It seems like kids are always wanting some new-fangled gadget that I don't understand at all. You'd think I'd be enough.

"It's a week today I saw the trash bag behind the pub," Lin says as we meet Deon. "Let's check it out."

Cautiously, I follow them to the dark area where Lin had first seen what she thought was trash. There it is again. Not much. Just a big plastic bag with its top tied shut. *Arrorr.* I sniff around it and detect a familiar scent. It isn't a bad scent at all, just a familiar one. I'm having trouble recalling where I've smelled it before.

"Do you think we should peek?" Sis asks Lin.

Grrrrrrr. Bad idea, girls. I growl a warning.

"I think Slobbers is telling us 'no,'" Lin whispers back.

"It's really none of our business," Deon tells them. "Listen to the big guy."

Both girls look at me. I turn and walk away, and I am glad to see them following right behind me. Deon takes one last glance over his shoulder then catches up, shaking his head.

"We'll come back again after school like last time," Lin whispers to Sis.

"Okay."

"Count me out," Deon tells them.

The girls look at him and giggle. "Scared?" Sis teases.

"Girls," Deon mutters walking away.

I totally agree.

~

After school, the girls come into our kitchen talking about the trash having disappeared once again.

"I'm really curious now," Lin is saying.

"I know," Sis says. "Maybe we could stake it out after Bud takes back his route."

"I dunno," Lin says. "Mom and Dad might not be too keen on the idea."

"So, who's to tell them?"

Both girls giggle. *This could be trouble.*

~

When Bud comes in the door, both girls scoot up to Sis's room. "Hey Slobbers," he greets me. "Wanna go for a walk? I need to see Mr. Brown."

Sure thing. Anything to get away from the gig- glers. We find Mr. Brown in his office.

"Hello Bud, Slobbers," he greets us with a big smile. "What brings you here this time of day? You're not going to quit, are you?"

"Oh no, not at all," Bud sits down in the chair Mr. Brown motions toward. I lay down beside him.

"So, you guys built a self-driving car for the robotics competition?"

"Yeah. It's way cool. We got one of those little cars we pedaled around as kids, motorized and computerized it. We even figured out how to di-

rect it from one place to another, almost like it has a brain of its own. Man, you oughta see that thing go."

"Wow, I hope you win!" Mr. Brown laughs.

"Thanks," Bud grins.

"You kids are amazing. I wish you'd get Deon interested in that club."

"I'm tryin'," Bud says. "Actually, I'm trying to get him to help me build a drone from a kit I bought. We're gonna be studying drones next."

What the heck is a drone? Well, if they build one, I guess I'll find out.

"A drone? Really? Go for it! You have my full support! Now, what can I do for you?"

"I was wondering how far back you keep papers," Bud says haltingly. "Like way back."

"Well, we have what is called an archives. It's online and has a copy of every newspaper we've published from day one. I'd be happy to set you up to have a look. What's up?"

"School assignment," Bud says. "Looking into the history of Serenity and the area."

"Ahhh, that sounds interesting. Come on. You can use the conference room."

"Thanks Mr. Brown. If I don't get everything I need today, may I come back?"

"Any time, Bud. I'm always glad to help."

Mr. Brown shows Bud how to search the files to find what he's looking for, then leaves us alone. Bud taps away on the keyboard, then stops and reads. He repeats this routine, making notes as he goes, and repeats it again. After awhile, he looks at me. "We better be getting home. Mom will be wondering where we are."

~

After dinner, Sis comes to Bud's room where I'm hangin' out and knocks on the closed door.

"Yeah?"

"It's me," Sis whispers. "I need to talk to you."

Bud opens his door. "What?"

"It's about delivering the papers."

That gets his attention. "What about the papers?"

"Well, it isn't the papers exactly," she says. "It's about what Lin and I saw again this morning behind the pub."

"What would that be?" he says impatiently.

"Well, last Thursday, Lin thought she saw something. Today we looked again and there was a big plastic bag all tied up, but we didn't see anyone."

"So? Was it near the trash bins?"

"Not really. It was hidden behind some barrels like no one wanted it to be seen. If it was trash, why was it hidden? Plus, it wasn't there this afternoon."

"Did you look in the trash bins?"

"Well, no. We...we really didn't think about it, to be honest," she admits.

"My sister the detective," Bud teases her. "Look, I'll get up extra early next Thursday and stake out the brewpub while you girls do the papers."

"Would you really? That would be great." Sis hugs him.

"I will. Now scram." He nudges her out of his room and closes the door, then sits down at his desk and studies the notebook he had at the newspaper office. I can't wait to find out what he's learning. I'll bet it's more about Cole.

~

On Thursday, Bud leaves before Sis and me after telling Mom he has some catching up to do

with the robotics project. Everything seems normal as we go about our routine, but as we start back, we see a figure coming toward us. This is strange. We've never seen anyone else out so early. Except whomever Lin thinks she saw behind the brewpub.

As the figure gets closer, I immediately know whom it is. *Woof.* I wag my tail enthusiastically. *Wow!*

The girls see the figure too. "Good morning," they say.

Wrapped in a big scarf and with a hat pulled low, the figure says nothing and scurries past.

I wag my tail. *Arrror. Not even a hello?*

The girls stop in their tracks and look at me and then at the figure moving on down the sidewalk.

"Do you know who that is, Slobbers?" Sis asks.

I do, and I wish I could tell her. I nod my head, though.

Sis and Lin look at each other.

"Let's hurry and see if Bud has left the pub yet," Sis says.

We race to the pub. Deon and Bud are huddled behind some big kegs. There is another big bag. *Arrror.*

"You know, guys, I'm going to take a peek," Lin says. We all creep into the dark space and Lin carefully unties the bag. "Will you look at this!" She pulls out a bag of flour, some sugar, and a big bag of coffee. "This doesn't look like trash to me. It's brand new. No one throws out brand new food! Do they?"

"This is really weird," Deon says. "There aren't any homeless around here, are there? That somebody would leave this stuff for?"

Lin carefully reties the bag and puts it back as she found it. "I've never seen any homeless people. You'd think they'd be talked about if they were around."

Bud says nothing.

"Well, it looks like we've got another mystery on our hands," Deon whispers.

~

Sis and Lin and I are waiting as Bud and Deon come into the kitchen. Seeing us, Bud motions for us to follow him to his room.

"What do you think?" Sis asks.

"Deon and I went by this afternoon, and the bag was gone. There wasn't anything in the trash bin either. Trash pickup is Friday, so it is curious," Bud admits.

"Well, we saw something strange, too," Sis says. "We were on our way back, when someone was coming toward us. Slobbers seemed to know who it was, but, of course, he couldn't tell us. He wagged his tail like he was happy to see whoever it was."

"Yeah, but we couldn't see," Lin added. "It was still really dark, and the person was all bundled up. We said 'good morning,' but whoever it was didn't answer."

"We watched for a minute, but he just kept on walking," Sis said.

I wag my tail. *Thump, thump.*

"What do you know that we don't?" Bud asks, looking right at me. *Oh, how I wish I could tell them.* "Do you think that person was a man or a woman?"

The girls shrug.

"It would have been a pretty small guy," Lin says, "but we couldn't see anything to tell."

"Uh-huh."

"What's next?" Sis asks. "Do we stake it out again?"

"I don't think so," Bud says solemnly. "I don't think it's any of our business."

"Ahhhh," Sis whines.

"Seriously," Bud says sternly. "Leave it alone."

"Yeah," Deon adds. "We don't want to get in the middle of another mess like the snails and the drugs!"

Woof. I agree.

Grumbling to each other, the girls leave Bud's room. "What do you make of it?" Deon asks.

"I dunno," Bud answers, "but I'm thinkin' we really ought to leave it alone."

"I have to agree with you there," Deon muses. "Dad and Mom are still on my case over our last adventure."

"I just hope the girls don't try to play detective."

Both boys roll their eyes. *Arrrrrf.*

~

Saturday is the day Bud collects from his customers. We usually go from door to door, one right

after the other, but today we pass by the Black's house. I look over my shoulder then at him. *Woof?*

"Don't worry Slobbers; we're comin' back."

After he has collected from everyone else, we return to the Black's door. Mrs. Black opens it to us.

Arf, arf. I wag my tail enthusiastically.

"Hello, Bud," she says. "Hello to you, you big bundle of love," she says, grabbing my cheeks and running her hands up to give my ears a good scratching, just like she always did when I acted as the go between for her and Cole. Suddenly she stops and looks at Bud.

He looks at her, then at me, then back again. "Is Mr. Black home?" he asks.

"Why, no he's not. Would you be wanting to talk to him?" she asks.

"No," Bud says quietly. "I'd like to talk to you." He hesitates as she studies him. "I...I know your son, you see...and I'd like to talk with you about him."

Her eyes fill with tears. "Well, you'd best be coming in then," she says, opening the door for us.

SLOBBERS

This change of seasons, as Cole calls it, sure is strange. It has gone from nice, crisp days with lots of sunshine to rainy and cold. Cole says it's probably snowing in the high country. That would be the land closer to the top of the mountains. He tells me it will be at our level soon enough.

Soon enough, indeed. In the morning, Cole is standing at the door calling me. "Hey Slobbers! Come look! Snow!"

Snow! This is the day I've been waitin' for! I push past Cole. White stuff is fallin' from the sky! It looks like the paper scraps, confetti I think it's called, like the stuff they threw at my hero ceremony. Only this stuff is so soft, you can't even feel it.

"Snowflakes," Cole tells me.

It drifts lazily down from as high as I can see.

I step out in it. It squishes between my toes just like mud, only it's not dirty. I stick out my tongue to catch some, but it disappears. I stick my nose in it. It's cold and wet. As I lift my head, a flake lands right on the tip of my nose. I look at it as best I can, being it's so tiny. It looks just like the fancy little papers Mom uses on her cookie plates. Doilies, she calls them.

But wait, it's gone. It just disappears. Like in a second! More land all around me, and more. *Wow. This is wild.* I race around in circles, loving the way my feet moosh through it. I roll over and over again, and then plow through it again with my nose. *Oooo, it's cool.* And very wet! It sticks to me in great clumps until I give a mighty shake, and it flies off.

Cole bends over laughing. I ram into him head on, and he tumbles to the ground with me. He packs a handful of it into a ball and tosses it. I chase it and try to pick it up, but it dissolves in my

mouth. *So, this is snow! Wow. What gobs of fun I'm gonna have in this stuff!*

Cole gets up and brushes himself off. I pounce at him. I wanna play some more! He grabs his pack of supplies though, and I know play is over for a while. He slings it over his shoulder.

"C'mon Slobbers," he says, starting down one of our many paths. "This is a good time to see if everything is as it should be."

Along the way, he shows me footprints of our friends. None of them looks quite like mine. If they do, they're a whole lot smaller. There aren't any at all that look like Cole's. We head down the path toward the ski resort.

"I need a look at those peaks," he says. "If they get too much snow too fast, it could mean trouble."

I'm happy just to romp around, in front of him, beside him, off in the woods, after him. Snow! How could it be trouble? I make big grooves in it with my nose, and then connect my footprints with the grooves. Grooves, footprints, grooves, footprints. *Wheeee. Boy, this is fun.* I wiggle down in it, roll over on my back wagging my tail back and forth, back and forth, and my legs, too, leaving great arcs in the snow.

"You're making a snow angel!" Cole laughs with delight. "How fitting for a Saint! Okay, my friend. We can play more later. Let's get back to business."

We get close to the ski area. He looks high and low and from side to side. "If that snow has been freezing and thawing, it could cause a problem," he tells me. "Especially," he says, "if some nitwit goes messing around in an out-of-bounds area. Out of bounds, where you're not supposed to be."

He cocks his head and listens. It is totally quiet. He nods his head. "So far so good."

I have no idea what a nitwit is but I'm sure he will explain it to me in time. I'm learning so many new words!

I cock my head as a rumbling noise sounds like it's coming toward us.

"Snowcats," he says.

They look like cars sitting on top of what look like caterpillars grinding through the snow.

"They're used to groom the cross-country trails," he explains.

Right. Got that. They sure don't look like any cat I've ever seen though. Heck, they're not even alive. They're more like the tanks the army guys drove when they were battling the snails. *Will reminders of that mess ever go away?*

Finally, we're ready to head back to our cave. Maybe we can play some more!

Now what am I hearing? It sounds like a really weak whimper. *Ooooowww, oooowww.* Uh-oh. I sniff the air. I smell what smells like the raw meat Cole cooks for us. Before he cooks it. Blood, I think Cole calls it. *Wooooo.* Why am I smelling it out here?

"What is it, boy?"

I push past him and race down the path, my nose plowing up the snow. I follow the scent as it veers off into the woods. The snow is getting harder to plow through, but we keep going. I dig my nose in deeper. The scent is stronger. Suddenly I see it, blood in the snow, lots of it, and the snow is churned up like something has been dragged through it. There are footprints too, big ones, nearly as big as mine...and like mine!

"What the..." Cole sounds alarmed. He pushes ahead of me, and then stops in his tracks. "Slobbers, stay," he says quietly. His face turns bright red, and I know it's not from the cold. I peer around his legs and see what looks like a huge dog laying in blood-soaked snow. He is crying weakly. There is a metal contraption clamped to his leg. It is rubbed raw and bleeding. I wince at the sight of it. Cole moves toward him carefully.

"This is a wolf," Cole says to me. "He's been caught in this...this steel jaw trap and is badly, badly hurt and just left to die." Cole moves closer. The wolf doesn't move. Cole says the wolf is of no danger to us.

"Slobbers, can you lie down against his back?" He pats the ground behind the wolf. "Down. Here." I stretch my length out against the wolf and can feel him shivering. I lay a paw over him and snuggle as close as I can hoping I can warm him with my own body heat.

Cole rustles around in his pack and pulls out a big roll of bandage. He takes out his knife, cuts off a long length then wraps it around the wolf's mouth so he can't open it. Then he motions for me to lay on top of the poor guy. I roll over on him as gently as I can, so my weight will hold him still.

"This is gonna hurt," Cole mutters. Shedding his mittens, he grabs both sides of the contraption, the trap, and with mighty effort pulls the jaws apart. He is sooo strong. The wolf lets out a weak yelp, then I feel him go limp underneath me.

"I'm going to dress his wound now, Slobbers." He takes some snow and wipes away as much blood as he can without causing the wolf more distress, then gets a chunk of the special moss out of his pack and wraps the wound, then he wraps it gently with more bandage.

"Stay," he says to me. "Stay with him for a few minutes." I keep my weight on him so he can't move, though I don't think he could if he wanted to.

Cole gets up with the trap in his hands and pulls the chain it's attached to out of the snow. He follows it well out of my sight. The wolf doesn't move. I can feel his chest rising and falling. I know he's alive. *How could anyone do this to an animal? To any living thing? I don't understand!*

Cole returns with the chain and a bunch more of the traps, the jaws all shut so they can't hurt any other animal. Or us. He looks grim.

"Think you can carry these for me?"

Of course, I can. He rigs a makeshift harness out of extra bandage and ties the traps on my back along with his pack. Then, ever so gently, he lifts the poor wolf in his arms, and we make our way out of the deep woods and back to our cave.

I never expected anything like this when he was fixing up the shelter, but thank goodness, he did. He makes a bed of pine boughs like the ones he makes for us on our overnight adventures and lays the wolf down. I lay beside our new friend while Cole gets him fresh water and one of my meaty bones. I don't mind at all. I ache for the poor guy. Why, I wonder again, would anyone want to do this to an animal? He's sure lucky Cole and I were around.

Once he seems to be breathing more evenly, Cole and I go in the cave for our dinner. Then he digs through his books. Finding what he's looking for, he turns up the light in his lamp and settles into his chair. I'm guessing it has something to do with wolves and traps.

Before turning in for the night, we go out to check on our guest. He hasn't touched his food or water. Like, that's no surprise. He's well protected from the snow and seems to be sleeping peacefully. I lie down next to him and lick his face. He sighs.

Cole smiles. "You want to stay with him?"

Aroo. I do. I know I wouldn't want to be alone. And it's not all that cold.

Cole brings me a big pile of my own bedding and waits until I get myself situated, so I can keep the wolf warm, then goes back into the cave.

This is totally new for me. Other than in my doghouse when I lived with the kids and Mom and Dad, I have never spent the night outside alone. When I wasn't with them, I was with Cole. I think about how comforting that had always

been. Wow. I think it's pretty great that maybe I can give some comfort to this guy.

I wake up when Cole pats my shoulder. It's still dark, and the snow has stopped.

"Sleep well?" he smiles. He pats the wolf, who seems to be sleeping soundly. He lifts up the bandaged paw, unwraps it, smells the wound, repacks it with fresh moss, and rewraps it.

"When he gets to feeling better," Cole says, "we're going to have to be very careful. He's a wild animal and probably won't take too kindly to us."

It takes him awhile to get to feeling better, though. Twice a day Cole changes the moss on his wound, and I stay with him during the night. One morning I wake up and see him looking at me. I'm way bigger than he is but, man, he's one muscular pooch. I wouldn't want to tangle with him.

Eeerf. He bats at me with his good paw. *Arror.* I answer. We study each other warily, then he reaches over and nuzzles me just like Bro and I do. *Wow. This is so cool!* I think we're gonna be friends.

Cole is watching from a distance. The wolf looks at him and gives the same response. *Eeerf Eeerf.* Very, very cautiously Cole comes closer and just hunkers down. He does this off and on throughout the day. By evening, he reaches out for the wounded paw. The wolf pulls it back defensively. Cole sits quietly and waits, then tries again. After awhile, he lets Cole take off the bandage. “Nice scab,” Cole tells him. “You’re going to be fine.” *Eeerf.* He licks Cole’s hand. Cole smiles.

With snow on the ground, it’s hard to hear people approaching, but I can smell their scent.

Bud and Bro! *Woof, Woof!* I bark at Cole.

“Uh oh,” he groans. “We have to head them off!”

I run ahead of him and pounce on Bro. We roll together in the snow. I even show him how to make snow angels. It’s so much fun. He’s loving it, too. After all, we are Saint Bernards.

“Hey Slobbers!” Bud says, laughing and watching us over his shoulder as he’s going on ahead. “Are you that happy to see us?”

“Bud!” Cole appears. “I wasn’t expecting to see you in this weather.”

Looking around Cole, Bud sees the wolf. “Wow! What’s this?”

“Injured wolf,” Cole says with a sigh. “Keep Little Slobbers back for a minute. He’s still pretty out of it, but I want to make sure. Slobbers?” He nods toward the wolf.

Bud watches fascinated as Cole and I approach our friend. *Hmmm, hmmmm,* he murmurs a little. I nudge him with my nose telling him the dog is my brother and the boy my friend. Just like Cole only smaller. I look at Bro, and he starts toward us.

"Is it s..s...safe?" Bud whispers.

Cole motions for him to come forward slowly. He and Bro are right next to us now and the wolf tenses. Bud steps back.

Cole reaches out and pats his head, "It's okay boy; it's okay." He relaxes a bit.

"Let's leave Slobbers and Bro with him to get acquainted, Bud. It may take a little longer with you, since you're human, like me."

Bud nods and they move quite a ways away, though I can hear their conversation.

"What happened? Bud asks.

"He got caught in a trap," Cole says angrily. "They're illegal and cruel, to put it mildly. I followed the chain on the one he got caught in and found seven more. I've got my work cut out trying to find whoever is responsible. I really want to nail the guy. It's like he's after an entire pack!"

"What will happen to the wolf?" Bud asks.

"When he's well enough, he'll go on his way."

"He needs a name," Bud says.

Cole laughs. "I suppose he does. Do you have something in mind?"

"It's not very original, but we could just call him Timber."

"Well, that's what he is. A timber wolf. So. Timber it is."

"Can I see if he'll let me get close? Bud asks.

"Let's try. Wolves don't much like people. Trapping is one reason why. They know who's doing it to them. They're smart. Like all dogs."

"Do you think they can sense those who would *never* do such a thing? Like you? And me?"

"Maybe so. He's let me dress his leg for several days now."

Bud and Cole come toward us very slowly.

Errrr. Errrr. Timber whimpers as Bud extends his hand.

"It's okay, Timber," Bud says softly. "I'm your friend, too, just like these guys."

He licks Bud's hand, then rolls onto his side and dozes off.

"He's still in the healing stage," Cole explains. "He lost a lot of blood. He sleeps a lot, but Slobbers stays with him to make sure he's okay. He's eating a bit now, and that's a good sign."

"Why do wolves have such a bad rap?" Bud asks.

“It’s complicated,” Cole sits back on his heels and studies Bud. “There’s this law called the survival of the fittest, and it’s kind of tied to the food chain. Smaller animals fall prey to bigger, smarter ones. We’re at the top of the heap because we can think. The rest survive by instinct and experience. Because we humans keep taking over wildlife habitat, they get their food from whatever source is available. In many places, it’s cattle and sheep, which are a cash crop for the farmers and ranchers who’ve taken the land, so they want to get rid of the wolves even though the government pays them for their losses.

“To make matters worse, when a kill happens, the photos that are seen are always gruesome and disturbing, but in actuality that’s the way it is in the wild. I’ve seen some horrible battles but stay out of them because they’re nature taking its course. In this case, however, it was done by man. For no apparent purpose other than to kill. There are no cattle or sheep outfits anywhere near. This guy was left to die a long, agonizing death. I know in lots of places trapping is still legal, but not here and I want to find whoever did this. Does that make sense to you?"

Bud is stroking Timber's head gently. "It does," he says. "What kind of guy would do this to an animal?"

"A not very nice one," Cole answers grimly. "So. Let's go inside and get something warm in us."

He gets up, and we all follow him into the cave.

Cole fixes Bud a cup of his special tea, and we all settle in. "So, what brings you out in this weather?

"I...I've something to tell you," Bud's voice is barely a whisper. "Please don't be mad."

Cole looks at him.

"I...I've talked with your mom."

Cole sighs and throws his head back. "Ahhhh."

"I had to," Bud hurries his explanation. "See, when Sis and Lin were subbing for me on my paper route, they noticed a big bag had been left behind the pub. They went back after school to see what it was, but it was gone. I figured it was just trash someone was too lazy to put in the bin. When it happened again, they opened the bag and found stuff you use sometimes, like coffee and flour. Then Sis and Lin saw someone hurrying down the sidewalk as they were finishing up their route. After their description, I put two and two together and figured it might be your mom. When I was collecting for my papers, your mom answered the door and seemed to know Slobbers really well, and he seemed to know her, too. So, I took the chance and told her I knew you. She cried a little and had us in, and, knowing you know both the Slobbers boys and me, she told me the whole story. We talked a long time. I really like her. I think maybe she likes me, too. I hope she does anyway."

Cole sits with his head in his hands. "I guess it was inevitable," he sighs. "Does anyone else know? Sis and Lin? Deon?"

"No. No one. But I did go to the newspaper office and read all the stories about you."

While the guys talk, I show Bro the still open scrapbook with the story clippings, and he sniffs the pieces of cloth that are still there. We understand each other.

"I know my dad could help you," Bud is saying. "I know he'd really like you and what you do here with the animals and all. Please let me tell him about you and at least meet with him."

"And if he doesn't like me, I lose everything," Cole says. "I don't know. My mom is the only one who ever believed me. Not the police, not my teachers, not the other kids, and especially not my dad. Why should yours be any different?"

"Because he's not your dad. He's my dad. Please Cole? It's really driving me nuts keeping all this secret, and I'd rather have it come out between me and you and my dad than by accident. Sis and Lin and Deon are all curious. Mr. Brown knows I've been looking at those old papers, and now your mom knows I know. It's just gettin' too complicated."

"I can't disagree with that," Cole nods. "So, what do you want to do?"

“Let me tell my dad the whole story, then I’ll bring him out to meet you. After Sis and I didn’t tell him about what started the snail mess, he told me I could always talk to him—no matter what.”

Cole sighs, rubbing his chin. “Okay,” he says. “You’re right. I suppose I’ll get found out some day. It might as well be by friends.” He pauses, then adds, “You know, you and the Slobbers brothers are the only friends I have. I thought I’d never have any.”

“Well, you do, and you can have more. I won’t let you down. Or Slobbers, he’s a huge part of all this, you know. Maybe it will kinda make up for all the trouble Sis and I and Deon and Lin caused before.”

“None of you caused it, Bud. Don’t ever believe you did. It was the guy at the health club, whoever he was. Something bad was bound to happen after he showed up. You just happened to get caught up in it. So, tell your dad, and come by when you can. Slobbers and I will be here tending to Timber for awhile.”

"Can we see him again before we leave?"

"Absolutely."

Timber is looking a little more alert. *Errrrew,* he greets us.

"This has been quite a day," Bud muses as he scratches Timber's ears. "I never thought I'd ever see a real live wolf up close and personal. Or get to pet one! This is pretty cool!"

"Just remember," Cole says. "Unlike the Slobbers boys, he is a wild animal and in the wild it would be a whole different story."

"There's a lot of whole different stories going around aren't there?" Bud says.

Cole looks at him and smiles. "So it would seem."

BRO

As we head home, Bud seems like a whole new person. We play fetch with snowballs, a lost cause because when I catch one it falls apart. *Arrrroff.*

Bud laughs heartily. The furrow between his eyes is gone. His step is light as he kicks through the snow. He even tries to whistle. If I could laugh, I would. *Snoooort.* I whistle better through my nose!

Dad is watching us through the den window as we get home. "Have a good walk?" he asks as Bud hangs up his coat.

"We sure did," Bud says cheerfully.

"I haven't seen you this cheerful in a while." Dad smiles. "It must be the brisk weather!"

Bud and I go into the den where Dad is sitting at his desk. "Dad, after dinner can we talk?"

"Of course. What's up?"

"It has to be between just the two of us. Not Mom. Not Sis. At least not yet."

"Sounds serious."

"It is."

After dinner, Bud, Dad and I go back into the den and close the door. I plunk down beside Dad because he gives the best ear scratches when he's distracted, and I love ear scratches.

"So, Bud, what's on your mind?"

"Remember after the snail stuff you said we could always talk to you and Mom? About anything? Is that still true?"

"Of course, it is, son. It's one thing parents do quite well—or should. Listening and helping." Dad smiles.

"Well," Bud blurts out, "this isn't really Slobbers."

Uh oh. Now my secret's out! What's gonna happen?

"This is his twin brother who didn't get into the growth hormone."

Dad's eyes widen, and he stops scratching my ears. *Oh noooo. What if they don't want me. What if they want Slobbers back? Would Cole take me back? Even if I'm not big like Slobbers?*

"Wait, wait, wait a minute here! Let me get this straight. Slobbers isn't Slobbers but his twin brother?" Dad says, sounding like he doesn't believe it. "Where...where is the, uh, first Slobbers then?"

"He's living with a guy in the woods. A really great guy. He's my friend, and he's the lost boy everyone says is dead but he's not. Cole Black." Bud's talking so fast he's stumbling all over his words.

"Whoa, wait a minute here. Slow down," Dad says. "Slobbers, who became a really giant Saint Bernard, is living with a guy in the woods? Where? How do you know this?"

"See, Cole is a giant, too. That's why he ran away from home. Some other kids gave him some hormone shots. A couple of football players stole a whole lot of doses. The guy who was dealin' figured it was them, but when they saw him comin' they grabbed Cole and shot him full of it. When the guy challenged them, they said it was Cole and why didn't he have Cole's blood checked. Well, when the story got out the police checked Cole's blood, and, sure enough, it was full of it, so they believed the footballers. And not Cole. They didn't even check the blood of the other guys who would have had it, too. But they were stars on the football team. Everyone said Cole took them because he was too small to play football, but he didn't even want to play football. When even his own dad didn't believe him, he ran away. But after all these years, he really wanted some company, so when he saw what was happening to Slobbers, he got Little Slobbers and we traded."

Dad is just sitting there, wiping his hand across his mouth, staring at Bud. So am I. What a story!

"And you know this guy?" Dad says. "How did you meet him, and where did you hear this story? Let's start with where you met him."

"In the woods. It was when Slobbers was really getting big. Too big for just about everything. Slobbers had gone deeper into the woods than where we play and met this guy. They became friends. You know how Slobbers seemed to be so smart? Well, it was Cole who taught him how to sit and stay and all that stuff."

"Uh-huh. Then?"

"Well, Slobbers kept growing, and of course the snails were growing, too. Because Cole had already been through it years ago, he suspected the drug peddlers might be back and that was what was causing it all. When Slobbers ran away and then we found him, it was in the woods. I sent Deon and the girls home to get something for a collar. That's when Cole came out of the woods and told me he could help get rid of the snails and that Slobbers could live with him, but I had to promise not to tell anyone about him."

"And you promised him?"

"I did. A solemn oath. I didn't figure anyone would believe me anyway, but an oath is an oath."

"Um-hmm."

"Anyway, he had figured out beer would kill the snails and taught Slobbers how to knock over the barrels and stuff with our help, so the beer would flow toward the health club and flood the streets and the snails would drown in it."

Dad waits for more.

"So, we knew Slobbers couldn't live with us anymore, and Cole wanted a companion so it seemed like a good plan. What I didn't know is that Slobbers had a twin that no one wanted, so Cole got him and trained him to be just like Slobbers so they could trade places and no one would know the difference."

"Uh-huh. And just how did he get Slobbers' twin?"

"His mom found out. She volunteers at the shelter over in Calamity sometimes, and she got him for Cole. They used him as a go-between, so Cole could stay out of sight."

"His mom?"

"Yeah. She's been helping him all these years. She's the only one who believed him."

"And you found this out how?"

"She told me. And so did Cole."

Dad sits there, studying Bud. "I'm having some trouble getting my head around all of this, kiddo. I guess it's leading somewhere?"

"Yeah. I want you to help Cole. He lives in this cave, see, and he's afraid to make it known he's alive. Even though his mom has been helping him, she's never really seen him. He thinks he's a freak and it's better that he stays where he is, but if the story he and his mom told me is true, then someone oughta' be lookin' for those guys who gave him those shots!"

"He lives in a cave? A cave?"

"Yeah, it's really neat. He's really fixed it up nice. He's even rigged up a shower for himself and cooks over a fire in a really big fireplace he carved out of the wall that keeps them warm. And he has books. Boxes and boxes of books. He...he didn't want me to tell you any of this, but I told him I was sure he'd like you and that he could trust you."

Dad cups Bud's chin in his hand and studies him for a very long time. It's almost like they're frozen in place. "Is this really true?"

"Absolutely. Every bit of it. Cross my heart. I wouldn't kid about anything this important."

"Well, I must admit, even with your imagination, this would be a pretty tall tale," Dad says seriously. "Now, I'm guessing you have a plan?"

"I'd like to take you to his cave so you can meet him and talk with him and see if we can't figure out a way to help him."

"And no one else knows about this other than his mother?"

"Right."

"Not Deon nor Sis nor Lin?"

"Nope. But stuff has been happening that's making things risky. Like Sis and Lin and Deon know something's going on, and they're gonna start asking questions. Or even worse, try to figure it out on their own. I...I just can't have that happen."

"This has a very familiar ring to it. I'm really glad you've come to me, son, I mean it. I'm really glad you felt you could and should," Dad says. "So. When do you suggest we make this journey?"

"How 'bout tomorrow? Before Cole changes his mind? Just tell Mom you're gonna join Slobbers and me for a walk. It's all true. Honest, Dad. The whole story. Honest."

"Okay. We can do that. You know we're going to have to tell her though, at some point."

"I know, but can we wait until after you talk with Cole?"

"I think we can do that."

Bud has tears streaming down his cheeks as he goes to Dad and gives him a big hug. He doesn't let go. Dad holds on to him, too.

"Thanks Dad. I knew I could count on you."

I lay with my nose between my paws *thwaking* my tail on the floor. I'm so happy I'm seeing this bond between Bud and Dad. It warms my heart. It's like the bond I have with Slobbers, but we sort of came by it naturally. I guess we're not as complicated as humans.

SLOBBERS

Dad! Dad! I smell his scent and race toward him with such vigor I nearly knock him off his feet. Dad! And Bud and Bro! I wasn't expecting them so soon.

Cole, who is checking Timber's paw, hears the commotion and comes running. He doesn't seem as happy as I am. In fact, he has a look of sheer panic on his face. I think he's really nervous about meeting Dad. I'm wagging and barking enthusiastically. I'm trying to tell Cole it's going to be fine.

"Hey, Slobbers!" Dad lets out a huge laugh. "Man, it really is you!" Bro joins the celebration as Dad takes us both into his arms and hugs us mightily. "You two are quite a pair!"

Cole is standing back, watching. Bud goes to him and tugs his sleeve. "It will be okay," he says.

"Right." Cole is watching Dad closely.

"What's this?" Dad asks, still laughing, as he spots Timber.

"Injured wolf," Cole says.

Never giving Cole's size a second glance, Dad extends his hand, "George White."

"Cole Black," Cole says totally enclosing Dad's hand in his huge one.

Dad looks at it for a second, then the two men burst out laughing. This is so great! Bro and I wag our tails as hard as we can as we feel the tension among our people melt.

"C'mon in," Cole opens the door to our cave. "I'll fix us some tea. Unless you'd rather have coffee."

"The tea is great, Dad," Bud offers.

"Tea it is, then."

Bro and I settle in next to Bud, who has seated himself on Cole's footstool.

"What's with the wolf?" Dad asks.

"Illegal trap got him," Cole indicates the pile of traps sitting on the floor. "I found eight of them. Someone was hoping to get the pack all in one fell swoop, I would guess. Now I've got to find out who."

"How did you find this fellow?'

"His name is Timber," Bud offers.

Dad smiles.

"Slobbers and I have a route we take through the woods and around the resort, keeping an eye out for anything out of place. If it's an injured animal, I bring it here and patch it up if I can. Anything else I let Mom...my mother know, and she gets word to whomever needs to know."

"Bud told me he's talked with your mother and that she told him your story. It's quite incredible."

"She's the only one who ever believed me," Cole hands Dad a cup of tea, then settles himself at his table. "I was reluctant to have Bud tell you for fear you wouldn't believe me either. But he thought you might be able to help..."

"Let the truth be known?" Dad asks.

"More than that. Bring them to justice. You see, when the great snail escapade occurred, I began wondering if the guys who did this to me might somehow be involved. Serenity is far enough out of the way, I can't see drug dealers just happening across it."

Bud's eyes widen.

Dad looks thoughtful. "You think the man who was caught didn't give up everyone involved? The authorities think he did."

"I think that guy gave up only enough to save himself from getting anything worse than he got. I think the people behind it are hiding in plain sight. I just have no way of finding out or proving it."

"Well, we have our work cut out for us then," Dad says.

As the two men talk, Bud looks like he's watching a tennis match like the ones we used to watch on TV. I'm afraid he's hurting his neck the way it's snapping back and forth. Dad is listening as Cole talks a mile a minute. I've never heard him talk so fast. I think he's trying to get everything he has to say said before he changes his mind.

"Okay," Dad says once Cole stops. "I know you're going to be reluctant to agree to what I'm about to suggest, but you and I can't get to the bottom of this alone."

"No police," Cole says.

"No police," Dad agrees, "until we need them. If what you think is true, then at some point we will. The current chief is a good friend and can be trusted, but we'll leave him out for the time being. Other than that, I'd like to make a suggestion. Because Sis, Lin, and Deon are all thick as thieves,

I'd like to enlist them and the help of their parents. And of course, Sarah, my wife."

"That's an awful lot of people." Cole sounds unsure.

"Well, Sarah and I don't keep things from each other, especially something this important. Deon's dad owns the newspaper and has lots of sources for additional information if we need them. Lin's folks run the art gallery and hear just about everything that goes on in the area and know just about everyone. It is a lot of people, but these four, I trust with my life. Also, the kids know something is going on and will really pressure Bud."

"I won't tell," Bud assures them.

"I don't want to put you in the position of having to lie to them," Dad says.

Cole nods in agreement. "Too many lies already," he says, "too many lies. Where do we begin?"

"I'm thinking I need to get up to speed on the news accounts of what happened. In the meantime, maybe you'd like my wife to talk with your mom? Would she like another mom to confide in?"

"Man," Cole says, "she's been carrying this around all alone for so many years..." his voice trails off. "Do you think your wife would be willing?"

"Absolutely," Dad assures him.

"I can introduce them," Bud offers.

"My mom's name is Molly. She knows about Bud and me. I'll let her know you and I have talked and get word to you after I've done so. She may be a bit hesitant and need some reassuring."

"I understand," Dad says. "In the meantime, I'll have Bud show me the research he's done at the newspaper to see what exactly those accounts say, then we can come up with a plan."

"Then you believe me?" Cole asks.

"Yes. I do believe you, and it's time to put an end to it once and for all. Serenity is our home, and the likes of these people are not welcome," Dad says emphatically. "When you get word to your mom tell her, too, that she doesn't have to stash supplies behind the brewpub anymore. We'll work out arrangements to get you what you need without putting her or your existence at risk until it's time."

"What about the kids?" Cole wonders. "Are they as trustworthy as Bud?"

"Bud?" Dad asks.

"We're all trustworthy," Bud assures them. "Even the girls. They're awfully nosy, but I won't tell them anything until you guys say it's oaky. I know for sure they'd like to help, though."

Dad and Cole smile at the comment about the girls. "In this case, maybe their being nosy is a good thing." Dad grins. "We'll figure out what we need them to do after we parents have talked."

Dad looks at his watch. *Oh no, it's time for them to go already?* As Dad stands, he asks Cole, "One last thing. Is there any chance I can get a look at Timber? I'm a city boy and have never seen a live wolf."

"Absolutely." Cole laughs, sounding happier than I've ever heard him. Except for when we were rolling in the snow.

We all clomp outside. Timber whines softly but doesn't seem afraid. "Be very careful. I don't want to frighten him," Cole says, apologizing. "Any day now he's going to take his leave, and I figure his natural distrust of humans will kick back in."

"I understand," Dad says. "What a handsome animal! How could anyone be so cruel? Finding that trapper is definitely on our list! Actually, it may be first."

Cole nods. "We've got to move on it while we might still find some clues."

Dad nods in agreement. The men shake hands, hesitate, and then actually hug. Dad pats Cole on the back. "Everything is going to be fine, Cole."

Back in our cave, Cole settles into his chair. I lie next to him and rest my chin on his knee. He stares into the fire, absently scratching my ears. His eyes are moist.

BRO

Mom is looking out the kitchen window as we tromp through the deepening snow. Well, Dad and Bud tromp. I romp.

She opens the door for us. “I was beginning to worry,” she says. “Where have you three been?”

“In the woods,” Dad says cheerfully. “Bud and Slobbers were showing me where the kids disappear to in the summer.”

“Is the snow deeper there? It’s been coming down here pretty steady for the past hour or so. I didn’t even have Slobbers to send after you with some brandy.”

The light-hearted mood continues through dinner, though Sis seems unusually quiet. After dinner, the kids head to their rooms to finish their homework. Mom, Dad, and I go to the den. I lie down at their feet and perk up my ears. I figure this conversation is going to be interesting, and I don’t want to miss a thing. *Man, I’ve been hearing a lot of interesting stuff lately!*

"The strangest thing happened today after you left," Mom says quietly, so that her voice doesn't carry. "Sis came to me with a very strange tale about stashes of goods she, Lin, Deon, and Bud are finding behind the brewpub some mornings. Then she and Lin saw someone scurrying along the sidewalk. She's wondering what to do. I'm wondering, too. I'm wondering if they're safe, even with Slobbers along. Should we notify the police? Is it any of our business? I just can't get the fiasco of the great snail escapade out of my mind."

Dad is shaking his head and smiling. He tells her about our adventure with Slobbers and Cole, and, as she listens, her eyes widen.

"So, what Sis and Lin saw were supplies Mrs. Black put out for her son? Cole?"

"That's it."

"That's incredible! He's alive? What's he like? Is he really a giant? And Slobbers is Slobbers' twin brother? I'm having trouble grasping all this."

"I did, too, when Bud first told me, but it's all true. The Slobbers boys are indeed twins, and

Cole is a very bright, well-spoken, and well-read young man. Nice looking, too, from what I could see beneath his beard and shaggy hair. He's a big man, but no bigger than an NBA basketball player. He's definitely no freak. His cave is spotlessly clean and even cozy. He is still bitter, though, about what happened to him. Mostly I think it's because no one other than his mother believed his side of the story. It broke his heart that his dad disowned him."

"But the drugs! Two football players gave him shots because they stole them and were afraid of getting caught? Why were they taking drugs in the first place? What kind of boys would do that to a smaller boy? How horrible! Can we help him? What should we do? What can I do?"

"He's going to tell his mom about our meeting and suggest she might like to meet you. My guess is she could really use a friend."

"Of course! I would love to meet her. But what else? That's hardly enough!"

Dad explains to Mom what he has in mind, including meeting with the Huangs and the Browns to explain everything and come up with a plan. Finally, Dad and Mom both let out huge sighs. I yawn. We all head to bed.

SLOBBERS

Arrrorrrrowwww. The moon is full. Cole comes stumbling sleepily from the cave to where I'm watching Timber howl and listening to other wolves answer in the distance.

"It's time, is it Timber?" Cole says softly, scratching his ears.

Arrorrrrowwwwww.

"Okay my friend." He opens the shelter gate and waits.

Timber comes to me and bats at me with his now healed paw while I nuzzle the thick fur of his neck. We look at each other. I understand he needs to return to his own, but I am, oh, so sad. I've come to love him and admire him. We have a bond. Not quite like Bro and me, but almost. We're brothers in our own way. He turns and passes through the gate, glancing back at us.

He gives a slight nod, then turns back to the path. *Errrrr.*

Cole and I watch as he disappears into the shadows.

As dawn breaks, we're already on our morning patrol. We see where Timber's footprints turn away from our path and head into the dense forest. I hope I'll see his footprints often, so I know he's okay. I think I'll be able to sense his presence, too, or maybe it's wishful thinking. I'm sure gonna miss him.

The snow is really getting deep. Cole is wearing what he calls snowshoes, which help him walk on top of the snow rather than sinking in up to his knees. I use my chest to plow through it, but it's getting pretty deep, even for me. Maybe Cole can make me some snowshoes. We near the edge of the woods just as the snowcats are finishing up their morning's work of trail grooming and the cross-country skiers are beginning to appear. Cole cocks his head listening. *What? Is there something besides the snowcats you hear?*

I cock my head, too. Right. It is different. It has a more annoying sound. A roaring of sorts, but not the deep rumble of the snowcats. I look at Cole questioningly.

"Snowmobiles," he says. "A recreational version of the snowcats. Smaller, louder, and a nuisance, but people love them. There are trails all throughout the mountains where people use them. Fortunately, none near us."

Well, this is a learning session for sure. I now know what snowmobiles sound like, what cross-country skiers look like, and how snowshoes work! One thing about living with Cole, I'm always learning something.

Home seems somehow empty when we get back. We've been so used to having Timber in the shelter, his not being there makes us both sad. It's good, though, that he left healthy and happy. I'm imagining the warm welcome he must be getting from his companions. I hope they've known all along we were taking really good care of him.

~

Cole is sipping coffee staring out our one window as I perk up my ears. *Arf.*

"Company? In this snow?"

We go out and greet Bro, Dad, and Bud. Darius Brown and Liu Huang are with them. Dad introduces everyone, and we go back into our warm cave.

"I didn't expect you so soon," Cole says. "What with the weather and all. Early storm. Got here sooner than I expected." Darius and Liu are looking up and down and all around the cave, their eyes wide.

"This place is fantastic!" Darius says. "You did this all yourself? Over the years?"

Cole nods. "Mom helped me get stuff. We'd agree on days she'd leave supplies behind the pub or where she would leave things she needed a car for so I could get them from the car to here without attracting attention." He looks at his hands. "I think it's getting to be hard for her, though."

"Your mom is so great," Bud chimes in. "She sure loves Slobbers! Both Slobberses!"

The men laugh. Bro and I do our tail-thumping routine.

"We wanted to come now," Dad continues, "to see if we can get a handle on who's been setting those traps. We figure maybe we could track them in the snow if they're still out there. By the way, where's Timber?"

"He went on his way. His pack was letting him know he was needed, and he let them know he was ready. We sure do miss having him around, but I think Slobbers is happy to be sleeping inside again."

Boy, is that the truth! Sleeping in the cold isn't so bad, but when the wind comes up, it gets pretty nasty. The shelter only blocks so much. Timber and I shivered together more than one night. I'm sure glad we had each other!

"So, what do you think Cole?" Dad asks. "None of us are really outdoorsmen. Certainly not on your level. How do we go about tracking this trapper?"

"I've been thinking about it a lot. Trapping has been illegal for what, three or four years? So, he must have had traps from before. That's going to be hard to trace."

"What about finding out who had permits when it was legal?" Darius asks. "I know farmers used to give bounties for wolves when their livestock was attacked. Maybe some trappers just continued on for the bounty money. Scofflaws."

"Is there a way to find out which farmers paid the bounties?" Liu asks.

“Back to the newspaper archives,” Dad says.

“We can check papers from Calamity and Chaos, too. They probably have stories we don’t,” Darius suggests.

“While you are working on that,” Cole says, “Slobbers and I will see if we can get up to the high country and have a look at some of the remote line shacks to see if there are any signs of life and activity. They’re emergency shelters for hikers and hunters, but hunting season is over so if anyone’s hanging out, it shouldn’t be hard to spot.”

“We should get you some supplies,” Dad says, “like a good pair of binoculars in case you see something and don’t want to get too close. And maybe a small camera. What else?”

“I could use some backcountry maps and a good compass.” Cole says. “If Bud and Deon could bring the maps and compass tomorrow after school, Slobbers and I can get started the next morning.”

“In that case, let me make a suggestion,” Liu says. “Why not let the girls do the research, or at least get started on it. I can run over to the sporting goods store in Calamity tomorrow and drop the supplies off with Sarah, so the boys won't have to waste any time after school. It gets dark so early now, I want them to have time to get home before dark settles in."

"That will work," Cole says. "Bud, I'll meet you and Deon at the edge of the woods, so you won't have to come so far."

"What time?" Bud asks. "We can be here by three thirty if we come straight after school."

Dad takes off his watch and hands it to Cole. "That should give them enough time to get out here and back while it's still light."

Cole looks at Dad then the watch. He nods. "Thank you. Thank you all from the bottom of my heart. Especially you Bud." He reaches out and tousles Bud's hair. "None of this would be happening if you weren't my friend."

Bud is beaming. Everyone is smiling as they say their goodbyes.

Bro and I are wagging our tails like crazy. *Oh boy, oh boy*. I nudge Bro; another adventure is brewing, and this is one we'll share. It's shaping up to be a beaut!

BRO

At Dad's suggestion, the families decide to have a spontaneous potluck dinner so everyone knows what the men have learned from their visit with Cole and Slobbers. I've never seen the kids so excited. Wow. Bud and Dad actually saw a real live wolf. And Slobbers is alive and living with a guy in a cave! And the lost boy isn't lost at all! Talk about adventure brewing!

"We want to meet Cole, too," Sis says.

"There will be plenty of time for that," Dad says. "He's not totally trusting, yet. That will come with our delivering on our promises and with time. You can divide up the research with the boys. You can decide among you who will search the newspaper archives, and who will search online for stories that may not be in our local archives. Both are equally important. Both you girls are good with details, and finding them is vital to our success."

“This is serious business,” Darius adds, “as we will be gaining Mrs. Black’s confidence. We don’t want to do anything to endanger Cole or her. Or any of us for that matter.”

“Whatever made me think Serenity was so serene,” Mom says, laughing. “Or that we’d be involved in all this mystery?”

“It’s because you have kids,” Bud says. Everyone laughs.

Don’t forget dogs; I thump my tail on the floor. *Arf, arf.*

~

I’m galloping through the snow ahead of the boys as we head for the woods. Snow is coming down again and piling up fast. It seems to be coming and going in spurts. Is that good or bad? Cole and Slobbers are hunkered down in the shelter of some rocks waiting for us. Deon sees Cole, and his eyes widen.

Slobbers romps out to meet us. We roll in the fresh snow for a minute, then settle down to listen.

“Cole, this is Deon.”

"Hi Deon," Cole greets him. "I feel like I already know you, having watched you guys most of the summer!"

"H...h...hi," Deon stares at Cole, his eyes wide.

Bud holds out the bag of supplies Lin's dad has purchased. "Mr. Huang wants you to make sure there's everything you need here."

Cole takes out the binoculars, maps, a compass and a small camera, a watch, and a few other things that are still wrapped.

He smiles and gives Bud his dad's watch. "Looks perfect," he says.

"You know, Deon and I have an idea that might make it easier for you."

"I'm listening." Cole smiles.

"Well, we belong to the robotics club at school where we're learning all about drones, so we bought a kit for ourselves with our paper money. We've been working on one that even has a camera. It can video everything under it. We think if we take it to the bottom of the ski area, we could

fly it up far enough to see if there's any activity at those line shacks."

"What exactly is a drone?" Cole asks.

Grinning, Deon sets down the backpack he's wearing and pulls out a four-legged contraption with spinners on each leg. *This thing flies?* It doesn't look anything like a bird, or a plane for that matter!

"It's battery powered," Deon explains, "and we handle it by remote control. The camera is pretty good and so is the battery, so it should be able to go far enough over the ridge to see what's what." He shows the remote to Cole. "See, we can see where it is on this screen."

"There's a clearing Slobbers and I use to watch the cross-country area not far from here. Do you think we have time to try it out?" Cole asks.

"Sure," Bud says. "The snow has stopped. We should be able to see something."

"Wait a minute," Cole says. "I think there's a road the Wildlands Bureau maintains near one of those shacks. Let's check the map."

The three of them huddle over the map. "There!" Deon points.

"It's the farthest, naturally," Cole says with a groan.

"Doesn't matter," Bud says. "Let's go."

Knowing time is getting short, Slobbers and I plow ahead of Deon, Bud, and Cole to make it easier and faster for them. Once at the clearing, Deon puts his drone in action.

Cole watches the boys. "This is really something!" he exclaims. "You two made this?"

Deon nods. "You can get really good ones in the stores, but they're kinda pricey. Bud and I wanted to see if we could make our own from the kit and add on some stuff ourselves. Like a stronger battery. This is a great test for it."

"Here, look," Bud tells Cole, holding the remote screen so he can see it. "Look," he exclaims, "there's the first one. No sign of life there."

Deon steers it on, allowing it to hover and looking for tracks for several minutes.

"Wow," Cole exclaims. "You can sure see a lot of territory with that camera! Look. There's the second shack...and the third."

The drone zooms closer, then Deon mutters, "Darn, I'm getting a low power signal. I've gotta bring it back."

"I'm sorry, Cole," Bud says.

"No worries," Cole says with a grin. "We didn't see any disturbed snow. That makes it much easier. I'm going to bet if there is anyone up there, they'll be at the fifth because of the old access road. If not, we can check out the fourth one on the way back. I know a shortcut to get there, and that's where Slobbers and I will start. With luck, that will be the place someone is hanging out. You guys are amazing!"

The boys high five one another and are grinning from ear to ear.

"We'll start out tomorrow morning." He points to a gap in the mountains. "Slobbers and I can head straight up there. From the crest of the ridge, with the binoculars, I should be able to see both shacks. You guys have just cut days off our trip! I expect we'll be gone a couple of days, maybe three if we see something to check out."

"Hey, we can charge the battery and get it over the ridge and keep track of where you are," Deon says.

"Perfect. Don't let it get too close to those last two shacks though. We don't want anyone spotting it if there is someone out there."

"Got it!" Bud says. "We'll just look for you and Slobbers, so we know when you're on your way back."

"Man, this is so exciting," Deon is putting the drone in his backpack. "I sure wish we could go with you!"

"Don't worry," Cole says. "I have a feeling we're going to have a lot of use for that gadget of yours."

The boys grin. Bud looks at his watch. "Yikes," he says, "we better get goin'!"

We all trek back to Cole's cave. The boys wish Cole and Slobbers good luck, and Slobbers and I have one more good tumble together. Then I join the boys, and we head for home.

~

"We found a ton of stuff in the newspapers about farmers offering money for wolves and stuff," Sis says enthusiastically at dinner. "And coyotes and cougars too! Lin and I don't understand all of it, so we gave everything to Mr. Brown to look over and decide what's important. We're gonna go back again tomorrow. Mr. Brown says he thinks more of it happened in other parts of the state than around here, so what Deon and Bud will be doing is pretty darn important, too!"

"That's great, Sis," Dad tells her. "Bud, did Cole have any idea of a time frame?"

Bud tells them about the drone and what they found and how they plan to keep track of Cole and Slobbers.

"Good job!" Dad says.

SLOBBERS

Cole spends the evening studying the maps, testing the binoculars, and figuring out how to use the camera. “These maps are great,” he tells me. “They’re Wildlands maps that show the contours of the land, where the cabins are, and where the roads are. It shows exactly where we need to go. It’s not a bad hike, if the snow up there isn’t too deep.”

As the sun comes up, everything seems magical with snow sparkling on tree branches and crunching under our feet, and we start out in good spirits—even if our mission is grim. I’m hoping the weather stays pretty much the same ‘cause Cole says we’re headed for some territory he doesn’t know well.

I’m having a fine time romping around in the snow and breaking far more trails than we need, but Cole is all business. As we get to the crest of the ridge, Cole takes out the binoculars and calls me to his side. He scans back and forth and back again.

I wonder what he sees. *Arrr?*

We go over the crest of the ridge and, keeping close to the sparse tree line, head for the fifth cabin. I sniff the air. I get a very weak whiff of man.

"I think we may have found something," Cole says very quietly. The cover is even more sparse as we move closer. "Don't leave my side," he tells me. Not a chance. My job is to protect him.

We get as close as we can, safely. "We're going to wait until dark," he says. "We'll be able to see if there is any light inside and if that disturbed snow around the cabin is recent or old. It can't be too old because it's only been snowing for a short while. Not long enough to cover stuff up."

A shiver runs down my spine, and it isn't from the cold. It's that whiff of man that bothers me.

"If the map is accurate," Cole tells me, "there should be an old Wildlands road not far from the cabin. If it's passable at all, a snowmobile might be able to get to that cabin without much trouble."

We find what's left of the road, and we can still see the cabin. There is no light coming from inside, so we move closer until we're so close we could knock on the door.

"If you hear anything, be ready to run," Cole tells me.

The snow has been tromped through enough that our tracks don't even show.

"Snowmobile," he says pointing out its tracks to me. "What's this?"

He's looking at some dark snow by the tracks. I sniff it. Blood! Not red like was around Timber, but definitely blood. I couldn't mistake that smell.

Cole takes a small cup from his backpack and scoops some of the snow into it. "Let's get back to our cover," he says.

Just as we reenter our sparse cover in the woods, we hear the familiar whine of a snowmobile.

"Whew," Cole says as we keep going. "We got out of there just in time!"

We watch as a figure parks the machine, gathers several bags tied to the back of it, and disappears into the cabin. In a few minutes, light shines through the window.

“No fire for us tonight,” Cole says. “Sorry Slobbers.”

We move as far as we can into our cover. He sets down his pack and rummages through it, finding our food and a couple of shiny blanket-like things. I sniff them and eye them with suspicion. Space blankets, he calls them, saying they’re lightweight and designed to keep us warm.

What the heck are space blankets? I look at them doubtfully. They’re not soft like real blankets. They’re stiff and make a crinkling noise when I move them around. They don’t look like they’d keep anyone warm in real cold, and, what’s more, keep two of us even moderately comfortable. Where’s Timber when we need him!

“Okay, boy, it’s you and me against the elements.” He lays one blanket on the ground, curls up against me, and tucks the other one over the top of us.

We’ll see.

~

It's still dark when we wake up. I'm surprised how comfortably warm I am. Without a fire. *Space blankets, eh? Okay.*

We make our way back to the edge of our cover. There is no sign of life around the cabin and no light inside, but the snowmobile is still there.

"We wait," Cole says, unpacking some more food for both of us.

Man, am I hungry!

I'm glad he remembered food, even though it's nothing like what we eat at home. I guess I'm so hungry because I must have walked twice as far as Cole did what with all my exploring. I love to snuffle out new places.

The sun is up and still no movement from the cabin. Cole looks at his new watch. "We'll give him some time, yet. It's early."

By the time Cole pulls out some lunch for us, I'm wondering if whoever is in the cabin is gonna to stay in there all day. Just then, the guy comes out. Looking around, he yawns and stretches and scratches his beard. He climbs on the snowmobile, the engine whines, and he speeds off with snow trailing out behind him.

Man, those things sure are noisy. And smelly!

I'm beginning to understand that things that smell bad usually are! I wonder who that guy is and what the heck he's doing out here in the middle of nowhere.

It reminds me of when I first found Cole. I liked Cole, though. Plus, he didn't smell bad.

I'm not so sure about this guy. Something about the whole scene makes me bristle.

"Come on," Cole tells me. "I want to have one more look."

As I snuffle everything, he takes pictures of the snowmobile tracks, the man's footprints, and what's left of the bloody snow. I'm nervous as he tries the door and it swings open. I push around him and look inside before allowing him to go in. *I don't want any surprises!*

He's smart, though. He peers in carefully before going inside. I nose my way around the various tracks some more while I wait and make note of the scents and listen for anything that sounds like the snowmobile returning.

Nothing. Whew!

Cole reappears, frowning. He hurries back to me. I'm relieved and worried at the same time.

"We struck pay dirt, Slobbers," he says. "Let's get out of here."

What's pay dirt? Is it good or bad?

Cole sounds happy but looks angry. Just like me being relieved and worried. It confuses me.

Our way back is easy. It's warmer, and the snow is melting. Our tracks disappear as we follow the trail back to the crest and start down the other side. Whoever is staying in that cabin will never know we've been there.

The snow is pretty much gone when we get to familiar territory. I'll be happy to get to our cave, warm up, dry out and have a decent meal.

Suddenly, I stop in my tracks.

"What's up boy?"

Bro, Bud and Deon are racing toward us, screaming at the top of their lungs.

"Where are you two? You're not supposed ta be out here alone! Or out here at all!" Bud is furious.

Cole turns his head toward an outcrop of rocks, and I notice a flash of color.

Oh brother. No wonder the boys are frantic. It's the girls.

I let out as deep a growl as I can muster. ***Grr-rrrrroowl!*** It's my way of scolding.

"Oh, boy," Cole squats down. "C'mon out you two," he says as the boys and Bro come to a screeching halt.

Bud and Deon are gasping for breath, and Bud is screaming. "We saw you comin' on the drone camera, and Deon and I were coming to meet you. They're not supposed to be here. I don't know how they found it. We followed their footprints in the snow and figured out what they were doing."

I'm gonna have to have a chat with Bro! Of course, he can't be with all the kids all the time, so I guess I shouldn't be too hard on him.

Sis comes bursting out from behind the rocks and leaps on me, nearly knocking me over. She's in drama mode, that's for sure. She's in trouble, and she knows it. "Slobbers, it's really you!" she cries. "It's really you!"

Lin emerges from behind the rocks looking scared, her eyes and mouth wide open.

"Whoa, settle down, Bud."

Cole pats Bud's shoulder to calm Bud, and waits until he's breathing more like normal.

Then he turns to the girls. "What are you two doing out here all alone?" Cole asks quietly.

"We were just really, really curious about you and where you live and all that," Lin says, hesitantly. "We didn't mean any harm."

"And I wanted to see Slobbers and...and we really feel left out," Sis stumbles over her words, still hanging on me, half-hiding from Cole and

Bud, who is still furious. "The boys always have all the fun!"

"How did you find your way here?" Cole asks.

Sis kept talking, stumbling over her words. "We...we followed Bud and Deon when they brought you your supplies. Then we waited until you were nearly out of sight, but we could see you enough to follow you here. Then we decided to wait until the boys were busy doing stuff for you and come back on our own. Especially since they had Slobbers with them. Our Slobbers. They're both our Slobbers. I guess they're both yours too... the smaller Slobbers. Whatever...it's all so confusing..." She's nearly crying.

"Um-hmmm," Cole says, studying the four of them.

I raise an eyebrow at Bro, and he gives me a half-apologetic and half-disgusted *arf.* The apology I accept, and the disgust I understand.

"Okay, ladies. There has been no harm done. Now you've seen me. You've seen Slobbers. Now. If you ever do something you've been asked not to again, anything at all, you'll just not be able to be part of any of this, and I'll have to tell your parents. Do you understand that what we're trying to do is dangerous? Very dangerous?"

The girls are shuffling their feet and looking down.

"Do you understand?" Cole asks again, sternly.

They nod.

"All right, then. Let's get something warm in us, and then I have some things that you, Bud, need to get to your dad."

"Yes, what, what?" all four are talking over one another, their remorse having totally disappeared.

Kids. They can be a handful. Fortunately, we Saints mature a lot faster than kids. Bro and I aren't even a year old, yet—and in people years, still younger than these kids—and we're expected to keep tabs on them. *It's no easy task; I'll tell ya that!*

After Cole gets a fire started and some water heating for tea, he gives Bud the camera and the cup with the bloody snow in it.

"Okay, now this is very important. I want to meet with your fathers as soon as possible, and Bud, tell your dad to keep this cup in the freezer until we've had a chance to talk."

"Yeah. I'm sorry, Cole. I didn't know the girls had followed us when Deon and I came out before."

Cole turns to the girls. "Have you been here other than when you followed Bud and Deon? I want the truth."

"No," Lin says. "Today's the first chance we've had. Honest. We were here only a few minutes before you and...and Slobbers showed up."

"All right. Now listen to me. You shouldn't be this far into the woods by yourselves. You should always have Slobbers with you. If anything should happen, he could go for help. Either find me or get to your homes. I couldn't live with myself if anything happened to any of you because of me. Do you understand?"

They all nod.

"Good. Now it's time for you to be on your way. It's getting close to your dinnertime, and your folks will begin to worry. We don't want that now, do we?"

"No," they all say together.

Cole and I walk with them to the edge of the woods and watch as they start through the meadow. He's shaking his head as we turn back toward our own home.

"I don't know, Slobbers, I just don't know. Having four rambunctious kids to keep on the straight and narrow may be our biggest challenge!"

Tell me about it.

BRO

"You sure messed things up," Bud snarls at Sis and Lin. "Why couldn't you wait like you were told?"

"And why would you go without Slobbers?" Deon asked. "You know we never play in the woods unless he's along. For the same reason Cole said. Like if something should happen that we couldn't handle!"

"Well, you guys always have Slobbers with you. He's supposed to be our dog, Bud, but the only time you leave him with me is when Lin and I are doing your paper route! Now that you're back doing it, we don't even get to see him in the morning! It isn't fair!"

"Fine!" Bud exclaims. "Fine. From now on, you feed him, you walk him, you give him his baths! Fine! C'mon Deon, I've had about all I can take of these girls!"

Bud and Deon run ahead.

"Fine!" Sis yells after them. "Fine! Dad usually takes him to the dog wash anyway! Fine! I'm gonna change his name, too! Two Slobberses is too confusing! I'm gonna name him Drool! So there!"

Drool? Ha! What kinda name is that? We'll just see.

I run ahead so I'm halfway between the girls and the boys. I've had about all I can take from any of them today! Drool? Well...maybe. Two Slobberses *is* confusing.

~

Mom is standing on the back deck as we get close to the house. Lin and Deon split.

"What is all the yelling about?" Mom asks sternly. "They must be able to hear you in the village!"

"Nuthin!" Bud mumbles.

"Sis?"

"Nuthin'. It's just brother and sister stuff."

Dad joins Mom, eyebrows raised.

"It's brother and sister stuff," Mom tells him.

"Right. Well, get inside and get cleaned up for dinner, brother and sister."

Bud and Sis glare at each other. I follow several steps behind.

Dad reaches down and scratches my ears. “Man, Slobbers, there are times I really wish you could talk!”

Bud is first to the kitchen and hands Dad the stuff Cole gave him. “Cole says he needs to see you and the Misters as soon as possible,” Bud says. “There’s a cup of frozen snow he wants kept in the freezer until he talks to you.”

“Frozen snow?”

“I think it’s blood or something,” Bud says. “It kinda looks like it.”

“Blood?” Mom gasps.

Bud nods.

Dad and Mom look at each other, but say nothing more.

~

Everyone is finished with dinner. Sis looks directly at me and says, “C’mon Drool, tonight’s your night with me.”

Bud winces.

"What's this?" Dad asks. "Drool?"

"That's what we were fightin' about," Bud says, sounding grumpy. "Sis wants to change Slobbers' name to Drool."

"Two Slobbers is too confusing." She glowers at Bud.

"It has nothing to do with that, and you know it! You want equal time with him. Well, fine. But you're never around. You and Lin are off learnin' cheers or how to shake silly pom-poms around. Or taking ballet lessons or other fluff. He's not interested in that stuff and couldn't go with you even if he was!"

"Whoa," Dad says, laughing. "You both have good points." He looks at Sis. "Bud is right; he can't go to your after-school activities with you. Anymore than he can go to robotics club with Bud. And Bud, two Slobberses is confusing. Maybe Sis would give up the equal time requirement in exchange for a name change?"

"That's not fair," they both cry.

"What would you suggest then? Either of you? Slobbers is doing what he does best. Making sure whichever one of you most at-risk is safe. That's Bud when he's taking messages to Cole. And that's you Sis, when you're delivering papers for Bud. We don't have this problem when you're doing things together, but for the moment, these times are few and far between. Don't you think we should all try to make the best of it for Cole's sake?"

"But Drool?" Bud asks, looking glum. "What kind of name is that?"

"Let's ask him," Dad suggests.

"Excuse me, please." Sis gets up from the table, glaring at all of us. "Drool?"

Whooo, boy. I look at all of them, and then push myself up and go to Sis.

When you come right down to it, two Slobbers-es *is* confusing, and Slobbers should be Slobbers. I kinda like the idea of having my own name. Now I can be my own dog. We can each be our own dog! Slobbers and Drool, the Stupendous Saints! *Yeah. It has a nice ring to it.*

"Well, I guess that answers that," Dad says.

SLOBBERS

Waking up after a night in our cozy cave is sure nice. I'm dry, there's no ice between my toes, and the smell of brewing coffee tells me Cole is already up.

"Hey, Slobbers," he greets me. "I've got a problem. I really want to talk with George, but I think we need to check out that avalanche area by the cross-country course. It's likely to have snow, even though everything here has melted. It's just enough higher."

He lets me out to do my morning stuff and waits. Looking at the sky, he frowns as snow begins to fall.

We return to the warmth of the cave. "I think we better go," he says. "If George and the other men get here, maybe they'll wait. I'll leave them a note." He writes his note and tacks it to the door where the men can see it.

I'm waiting for him as he picks up another bag from the table. "Now, for you my fine furry friend. Before we head out. This could be important. Mom sent you and Little Slobbers a present," he says, grinning.

I am so surprised when he turns toward me. It's a barrel. *A real honest-to-gosh Saint Bernard brandy barrel! Wow!* It's attached to a really cool collar.

He bends over me and puts it around my neck. I give him the biggest kiss lick I can muster. *Man, does this make me official or what?*

It must be full, too, guessing from the weight. The one the kids had me wear never had anything in it. This must be a really serious trip we're about to take!

What's this? He sets a smaller version of my barrel outside the door. *It's for Bro! How great is that?* I nudge it with my nose. Yep. It has brandy in it, too!

Cole puts on his snowshoes, and we begin our trek up the trail. I'm feeling mighty proud. I'm wearing my barrel as a badge of honor. I'm so proud to be Cole's dog and friend and companion because he's such a great guy.

He cares so much about everything. He understands weather and how avalanches happen without warning and how awful it is when people get buried in them. He's told me they can die because they can't breathe beneath a ton of snow on top of them. His sense of what's around him is so good, I'm really worrying. We wouldn't be doing this if he wasn't worrying, too.

The snow is deeper as we get closer to the ski area. Suddenly, Cole stops and cocks his head, listening. I hear it, too. It's a huge roar! I want to cover my ears with my paws.

Cole is moving as quickly as he can, what with the deeper snow and snowshoes and all. I'm plowing along in front of him to where we can see the cross-country course. Even though it's early, there are quite a few people already there.

Funny, they're not moving. Wait! It's because they're all looking toward the roar.

Oh no! Snow is cascading down the mountainside at breakneck speed, hurling rocks and trees every which way like they were no more than peb-

bles and sticks. It sweeps over the people, sending up huge billows of snow and rubble. Skis and poles fly everywhere. Off to one side, a snowmobile is flipped over, but lucky for its rider, neither are buried.

"C'mon, Slobbers!" Cole shouts, "We've got to dig them out! Fast! Time is everything."

We race as fast as we can to where we see signs of people. Cole claws at the snow with his hands, sending me on to where not much can be seen. He knows I can sniff them out. I surprise myself at how easy it is to find the scent of a human! I start digging, too.

Man, though digging in snow isn't as hard as in dirt, I seem to be having to dig awfully deep! I find a sleeve and tug until a person emerges, then on to the next 'til I find a boot or a pant leg. Cole comes behind me, making sure they're free and breathing; then we move on to the next.

If someone doesn't come around quickly, Cole gives them a slug of brandy from my barrel. "It warms their innards," he tells me. "Keep going. We've got to get them all out, then we're going after that snowmobiler!"

Oh no! The rider has righted the snowmobile and is getting on. Cole runs toward it even though the snow is hampering him.

WOOF! Woof! Woof!

Now what? It's Bro racing toward us as fast as he can.

"Cole!" A familiar voice is shouting at us. It's Dad. "Get out of here! We'll handle it!"

It's Dad, Liu, and Darius, with Bud and Deon close behind.

"Slobbers, get him and go!" Dad yells. "Get Cole out of here!"

I sense the urgency and plow my way toward Cole, who is nearly at the snowmobile. I look over my shoulder. A few people are staring at us with open mouths. I know what it is. Our size. I grab Cole's collar, wrestle him to the ground, and drag him away.

"Stop, stop! What are you doing, Slobbers?" he yells at me. "I've gotta get him. I've got to!"

I keep dragging him, fighting his efforts to get away. I'm very strong. Very strong and, as strong as Cole is, he's no match for me. He sees Dad coming toward us and quits struggling. *Whew! He was wearing me out!*

"We'll get him, Cole, we'll get him. You and Slobbers get out of here before people realize what they're seeing is real. We'll see you back at the cave."

Exhausted, Cole nods in agreement. He drops his head for a minute and catches his breath. Slowly, we make our way back to the woods and our own safety.

I look back over my shoulder. Dad, the men, the boys, and Bro are helping the skiers, right

down to giving them brandy from his barrel. *That's my brother!*

Now what? I hear something faint, not a roar like before, but deeper and even more menacing. *Oh no!* Is there more snow coming down the mountain?

No. It's more like growling. Cole looks toward the sound. His mouth drops open. We can see the snowmobile, and I'm guessing only we can see it. Because of where we are. It's surrounded by...a pack of wolves? Wolves! It's like they're toying with the rider. Batting at him. Nipping at him. Picking him up and shaking him. Like a cat does with a mouse.

They're not attacking him like they want to kill him or anything. He swats at one, and another comes at him from a different direction. *Oh, wow!* He tumbles off his ride! The wolves circle him. Then the biggest one straddles him and tears at his clothes. The others join in, sniff a bit, tear off a bit, and then turn and leave, taking pieces of clothing with them. His hat. Maybe a glove. Is

that his boot? Why haven't they attacked him? They just take what they've ripped from him and wander off.

The big wolf steps on him and over him and joins his pack.

Cole and I look at each other in wonder.

"Timber," he whispers.

Rrrrimber. I agree.

The man doesn't move for several minutes, then finally wallows his way to his snowmobile, manages to get on it, and, after some effort, gets it started. He disappears over the ridge.

We hear a new sound. A familiar one and a welcome one. The snowcats. Cole and I turn and head back to the cave.

~

I'm chewing chunks of snow from between my toes when I hear the squishing of snowshoes outside the cave. I thump my tail, letting Cole know it's his friends.

Dad is dusting snow off himself as Cole opens the door.

"Where's everyone else?" Cole asks, looking for the others.

"Well," Dad says accepting a cup of hot tea, "being a newsman, Darius figures he has a story to write. Liu, Deon, Bud, and Drool are providing your cover."

"Drool?" Cole raises an eyebrow. So do I. They've given Bro a new name? Drool? That isn't a very Saintly name. Of course, neither is Slobbers. It is kinda neat though. He's now a hero in his own right by taking my place helping the avalanche victims. After all, he's my twin, not my shadow. *Go, Bro!* Drool.

Dad laughs. "Sis got in a bit of a huff the other day and decided two Slobberses was too confusing, so she decided to name our Little Slobbers Drool."

Cole laughed. "Drool. Slobbers and Drool. Now that's a pair. Has he accepted it?"

"Quite well, actually. Hopefully, we won't have to explain it to anyone until the reason becomes obvious. For all practical purposes, Drool will be Slobbers for the avalanche story, but from then on, 'Look out world, here come Slobbers and Drool!'"

After the men stop laughing, Cole asks, "Did you see the snowmobile and the wolves?"

"Wolves? Snowmobile? I guess we were too busy to notice, but I didn't hear or see anything. What happened?"

Cole tells Dad what we saw, and his suspicion the snowmobiler set off the avalanche because he ran rather than trying to help. He also suggests he might be the same guy we saw at the line shack because that seemed to be the direction he was headed as he disappeared.

"Ahh," Dad says, smiling, "the plot thickens..."

BRO

Mom, the men, and the boys are chatting in the kitchen as Dad comes bursting in.

"Man, it's cold out there." He blows on his hands, which are red from the cold. "Hi, guys," he greets them. "I didn't expect to see you quite so soon."

"You've had quite a day," Mom says. "The men are telling me how they didn't want to muddy people's memories as they got hold of their senses, so they sent you, Cole, and Slobbers packing."

"I think now they'll mostly remember Slobbers as being the dog who helped dig them out. Which of course he was," Darius says.

"It's Drool now." Dad laughs. I thump my tail.

"Drool?" the men say in unison.

Dad explains how I got my new name. They talk about the story and say I'll be referred to as Slobbers and decide it's no big deal because no one outside of our families knows about my new name and why I have it.

Dad tells everyone about the snowmobiler and the wolves.

"Man," Darius says. "I'm sure glad no one else noticed any of it. Explaining that away would have been a greater chore than explaining Cole and Slobbers!"

"Be glad for small favors," Liu adds.

"What's next?" Mom asks. "It seems the intrigue never ends! It sounds to me as if this could be getting dangerous. For everyone."

"We'll be okay," Bud says, "as long as we have Drool with us and the girls stay home."

"I'm going to get Cole a phone," Dad says. "It will make things much easier, and you boys won't have to be messengers. There will be plenty of other things for you to do."

The boys frown but say nothing.

"Good idea," Darius says. "From what the kids have found in their research, I think our friend may have stumbled across something far more sinister than we ever thought."

"Oh my," Mom sighs. "How did this village ever get the name of Serenity?"

"Wishful thinking," Liu says with a grin.

SLOBBERS

After dinner, Cole and I are relaxing in front of the fire. He's reading and I'm watching the flames dance. We hear a thump at the door.

"What the...?" Cole gets up, opens the door a crack, and peers outside. Poking my head around his legs, I see a heap of stuff. This isn't stuff from his mom. She wouldn't come out here alone at night, would she? Heck, she doesn't even know where we live! Curious.

Looking closely, I see a glove, a hat, maybe part of a scarf, and yes, an actual boot! We look out into the night and see a pair of shining golden eyes watching us.

"Timber!" Cole exclaims.

He squats down, and I lay down beside him. Our giant friend comes to us.

I raise a paw in greeting. We nuzzle each other happily.

Cole puts his arms around Timber's massive neck and buries his face in his coat.

"Oh, my, Timber. You got this for us. What can I say? Thank you. Thank you."

They look deeply into each other's eyes. *Talk about bonds!*

Rorowww.

He licks Cole's face and mine, then turns and fades back into the night.

~

Cole is sitting in his chair staring at the pile of torn clothes. I nose them so I can remember the stink. It's not even a scent, it's so foul. It's a stink.

The familiar knock tells us Dad, Darius, and Liu have arrived. "Boy, am I glad to see you!" Cole greets them. "Look at this!"

"What is it?" Liu asks. "Looks like the local ragpicker paid a visit."

"The ragpicker was Timber," Cole says. "He just dumped it at the door, said hello, then went on his way."

"Leave it be," Darius cautions, "we don't want to mess up anything that might be evidence. If the snowmobiler is the same one you saw at the line shack, there could be DNA that would tie him to trapping illegally as well as setting off the avalanche. Wolves aren't dumb. They could probably tell from his scent he was one and the same and decided to lend a hand."

"Or a paw," Liu says with a grin. "Listen, I know some people at the university who might do me a favor and run this stuff through their lab."

"But what will we compare it with?" Cole asks.

"For starters, we can see if that frozen snow in my freezer is animal or human blood. If it's human, we might get a match. There could be something on that pile of traps you have, and, of course, this clothing. I'd guess there are some hair samples in the hat. Probably sweat, too."

Cole stares at him for a minute then goes to a stack of books and pulls out the scrapbook with the cloth scraps pressed inside.

"This may sound crazy," he says, "but could we have these checked and see if there's a match between either of these chunks of football jersey and this new stuff? I tore them off the guys who dosed me and, for some reason, decided to keep them. Imagine. All these years."

Liu takes out his handkerchief and folds the pieces of jersey into it.

"What's this?" Darius asks, leafing through the book. "Are these articles about you?"

Cole nods.

"Hmmm." Darius is smiling broadly. "Names. Now we're getting something to work with!"

The men are all grinning.

Yes!

BRO

I wish the men had taken me with them when they went to see Cole. Deon and Bud are closed away in Bud's room working on their drone. Mom is fussing in the kitchen. Sis and Lin come in and climb up on the counter stools. I flop down close, so I can listen.

"Mom? Have you ever met the Blacks?"

"I've met Mrs. Black," she says. "Why do you ask?"

"Well...we thought it might be nice if we could take Drool to visit once in awhile. Because she knows him. Maybe she misses him since he came to live with us."

Mom smiles. "How thoughtful. Why don't I call her tomorrow and ask if she'd like to see him you can go after school."

The girls look at each other, and, under the counter where Mom can't see, they give each other a thumbs-up.

Oh boy, what are they up to now? I have a feeling I'll need to keep a close eye on them.

~

I really like Mrs. Black, though I don't know her very well. She always made sure there were goodies for me when she left things for Cole behind the pub.

She opens the front door for us and greets the girls warmly and gives me her usual hugs and squeezes. I curl up at her feet as she and the girls sit down for something warm to drink. It is cold outside; that's for sure! The girls surprise me. They haven't let out one giggle. Whatever they have in mind must really be serious.

"We only met Cole once," Sis says, "and Bud got really mad at us, but we really wanted to meet him."

"We really liked him," Lin adds. "You must miss him terribly."

They chat about what he was like as a boy and who his friends were and if any of them are still around. What he liked to do. He definitely did not want to play football!

Mrs. Black answers everything they ask quite happily. She seems to enjoy having the girls there and she definitely enjoys talking—especially about Cole.

Time flies by, and we have to end our visit, but I'm really happy Mrs. Black wants us to come back.

She has the best dog treats ever. Cole told me she makes them herself. Is that neat or what? Just for me! And now, probably for Slobbers, too. She must make giant size ones for him!

SLOBBERS

The weather is so cold, neither Cole nor I want to stay out in it any longer than we have to. At least, it's not snowing.

Passing the cross-country ski area, we see that the damage from the avalanche hasn't been fixed, so there are no people there to worry about. Cole cocks his head, listening. I do, too, but I hear nothing. *What a relief!*

We're surprised to find Bro, Bud, Deon, and the men waiting for us when we reach home.

"Hey, guys!" Cole greets them. "What brings you out here in this weather now that I have this fancy phone?"

"Because you don't answer it," Darius says laughing, as we all go in and gather around the fireplace. "Besides, we have some news and some ideas to discuss with you."

Cole brews up some strong, hot coffee for the men and his tea for the boys. Everyone welcomes it, warming their hands on the cups. Bro and I snuggle with the boys and settle on the floor to listen.

"My friend at the university has run the DNA tests on the clothing from the snowmobiler and, sure enough, your hunch was right." Liu says. "Also, the snow you froze had his blood in it. Probably cut his hand unloading his traps or something. His DNA also matches one of the scraps from the jerseys you gave us. The problem is, we don't know which jersey belonged to which boy."

Cole brightens. "Not a problem," he says, looking at me. "Did you bring them with you?"

Liu shakes his head no. They all groan.

"Wait," Cole says. He gets one of the traps and the scrapbook and sets them in front of me.

"Each swatch," he continues, "was pressed between different pages. Slobbers will know."

Oh, yeah, I will! I sniff the first scrapbook page, then sniff all over the traps plus some of the scraps of clothing from the snowmobiler the men had left with Cole. Nope. I go back to the scrapbook, sniff the second page, and return to the traps and scraps. ***Woof! WOOF!!***

The men look at me in amazement. *Hey, the nose knows!*

"Now," Darius says, "are you sure you've always had them in the same place?"

"Positive." Cole answers. "I put them in there just before I left home. There were pictures of each of them but never together, so I put each with the picture of the guy it belonged to. I never looked at it again until I met Bud and it all began coming back. See? I even traced the outline of the piece on the page, so I'd remember which piece went with whom. I don't know why I did that. I think at the time I was so angry, I vowed to get even, and doing what I did seemed a good idea." He chuckled softly. "So you see, this guy on this page is the poacher. Seth Craven. It figures. He was always the biggest bully."

"Do you think he's connected to the guy who was pushing at the club last summer?" Liu asks.

"I expect so." Cole says. "It sounds like both he and Damian, the other boy who attacked me. Seth could have filled the pusher in about a lot of the local people, let the pusher take the risk, and then taken his cut while remaining out of the picture. Damian could have done the same thing. He could actually be part of it, too. He was the smart one. They were really tight. I don't have a clue where he might be."

"Well, if all you tell us is accurate," Darius says, "your poacher is Seth Craven, and he has a rap sheet as long as my arm. Poaching wolves in the high country above Chaos where cattle and sheep range freely in the summer, and selling drugs all over the state. Why he isn't behind bars is beyond me."

"What's the other guy's last name?" He looks at the article in the scrapbook. "Price?"

Cole nods, and I *grrrrrr.*

"We'll get to him," Liu promises.

"How do we go about getting the Craven character?" Dad asks. "It would seem he's pretty slippery."

Bud and Deon have been listening along with Bro and me. Finally, Bud speaks up. "We could see with our drone if the snowmobile tracks at the avalanche site go all the way to the line shack."

The men look at him.

Deon grins and says, "Bud and I have been working on improving it since we were out with Cole."

"Yeah," Bud says, "we've put a better camera on it and increased its power so it can go farther and higher."

Cole winks at them.

~

Darius has borrowed snowmobiles from the resort. Our first stop is the foot of the mountain, where the boys fly their drone along the path of the snowmobile's tracks. It just keeps going and going, so we slowly follow it. Because there has been no new snow, Bro and I are having no trouble keeping up.

We all stop just beneath the crest of the ridge, but the boys keep the drone going. Wow. We see the line shack. Suddenly a man runs out of the shack with what looks like a long stick in his hands. A gun! He points it at the drone, and we hear a loud *craaaack,* then another one, and another, kicking up snow all around us. The drone stutters, shutters, and flutters to the ground. Bro takes off at full speed to retrieve it, and everyone yells, "DROOL! NO!"

I echo them with great, huge woofs and take off after him. *He's in danger. It's up to me to save him! He's my brother!*

The man raises the gun again and points it at Bro. *Craaack! Craaaak!* Snow is kicking up all around Bro! I take a flying leap and land on top of him, letting my momentum push us into the snow to hide us from the shooter's sight. *Whew! That was close!*

"Nooooo," the boys cry out, racing after me. The man lifts the gun again! *Wait!* He lets out a scream, and the gun flies up in the air as he falls to the ground with...with *yes*!

It's Timber!

He nails the guy. His pack surrounds them. He looks up at me, as he straddles the man. I know what he wants to do, and I also know he won't.

As I get off Bro, I signal Timber to keep the guy pinned.

Bro raises his head and looks at me, woofing a thank you. He tells me he's sorry he didn't wait for a command and maybe messed everything up. He gets to his feet, looks himself over, and shakes himself off. The shots missed. Thank goodness! The boys go over every inch of him, then hug him so hard he yelps.

I watch with satisfaction. Bro knew what he needed to do and didn't hesitate. I am soooo proud of him. *He's my brother through and through!* Just a bit smaller.

The men, having left their snowmobiles at the ridge, see what's happening as they stumble up to us. Timber is still straddling the guy.

Now what?

"Slobbers?" Cole says quietly.

Got it. I trot the rest of the distance to where the pack is waiting. The downed man stares at me. Timber is a huge wolf, and I'm bigger than he is. I take a great deal of pleasure seeing sheer terror on this man's face. Good. There's nothing I'd like better than to let Timber and his pack have him for dinner, but we both know that can't happen.

Timber steps off him and comes to me. We nuzzle each other. I love this guy. I nod to his pack, pick up the gun, and we go our separate ways, leaving the guy half-buried in the snow and shivering, but I wager it's not from the cold..

Liu is waiting with his handkerchief in hand and takes the gun from me.

"Great job, Slobbers." He scratches my ears.

Darius stares wide-eyed at the departing wolves. Deon and Bud are checking the damage to their drone. Dad is watching the man who is still on the ground, not moving.

"He's okay," Cole says. "Slobbers would have told us if he wasn't. Let's get out of here before he collects his wits."

"I wonder how much he actually saw," Dad says.

"It may not matter," Darius joins us. "If we can get the video from the drone, it will show the path from the avalanche site to the shack, and we've got the rifle with fingerprints. Plus the photos Cole took before with the traps and pelts."

"Police?" Cole groans.

"Maybe the Wildlands rangers can handle it," Darius says. "This is Wildlands territory, and they own the ski resort. I know the regional director. Nice young fellow named Jamie Holsom. I'll talk with him. I imagine he'd be delighted to take it to the police."

The men and boys get on the snowmobiles. I bump shoulders with Bro and *rufff* at him to let him know I think he is really brave, and I'm proud of him. He knows he was the one that had to go after the drone, so I wouldn't be seen. I don't think anyone anticipated a gun. Side by side, we wend on our way back to the cave.

BRO

I'm lying in the kitchen sniffing the wonderful smells floating all around me. Mom is preparing for something called Thanksgiving. It's a special day, I'm guessing, from all the food I see. They must eat a lot. I guess it's only a couple of days away.

Sis comes in and climbs on her stool. "Mom, I've got an idea. Mrs. Black is spending Thanksgiving by herself because her husband is going off to some sort of brewpub competition. Why don't we invite her to come and eat with us? We always have heaps."

Mom stops and looks at her. "Sis, I think that's a wonderful idea! Why don't you and Bud take Drool and go invite her!"

I'm always happy to visit Mrs. Black. It's actually a pretty nice afternoon. The sun is out. It's not too cold. Everyone is in a very good mood.

Mrs. Black answers Bud's knock. "Well, land sakes!" she exclaims. "I surely didn't expect to have visitors this close to the holiday! Shouldn't you be home helping your mother?"

"We've come with an invitation," Sis says gleefully.

"Yeah," Bud says with a grin, "we'd like it very much if you'd come have Thanksgiving dinner with us."

"'Cause Mr. Black's going to be away and all," Sis says, "No one should have to spend it alone, and we always have tons of food."

Mrs. Black stops scratching my ears. The kids look at each other as she turns away, her eyes getting misty.

"How very nice," she says, her voice quivering. "How very, very nice."

"Is that a yes?" Bud asks excitedly.

"I'd not like to put anyone to any extra work," she says.

"You won't," Sis assures her. "We'd really, really like very much to have you."

"Then I accept." She smiles. "Is there anything I might bring?"

"Just yourself and a huge appetite," Bud and Sis are both grinning.

A huge appetite? I can't wait to see what this Thanksgiving thing is all about!

~

It's Thanksgiving Day. Dad is home. Mom has been in the kitchen all day. The kids are wearing clothes other than jeans and T-shirts. Sis is putting dishes and silverware and glasses on the table. Bud and I are looking out the window.

"She's here; she's here!" he shouts as a car pulls into the driveway.

"Perfect," Mom says hurrying to the door. "Hello, Molly!" She hugs Mrs. Black. "We're so glad you could come. The kids and Drool have been so excited."

"Hi, Molly," Dad steps forward, "I'm George."

"You're just as Cole described you!" Mrs. Black laughs and gives him a big hug. "Thank you so much for having me!"

She hugs the kids, then gives me several of her special treats. *Hey, this Thanksgiving thing is all right!*

Everyone is seated around the table. "We have a family tradition," Mom says, "where we all tell what we're most thankful for each year. I hope you'll join us, Molly. Bud, will you begin?"

"Man, it's hard to know where to start," he says softly. "For good friends. Old and new..." he glances at Mrs. Black, "even though there's one who isn't here with us today..."

SLOBBERS

I hear the unmistakable roar of a snowmobile. This sounds like more than one! There's a pounding on the door. It's Bro and the gang.

"Hey guys, what's up?" Cole sounds surprised to see them.

"Deon and I have an idea and want to bounce it off you," Bud says excitedly.

"Well, come on in, and fire away."

"Dad and the Misters are wondering if the guy is still at the line shack, and, if so, how do we keep him there until the Wildlands rangers can get to him?" Deon says. "We fixed the drone and made it even better. We know we can find out if he's still there. If he is, we're wonderin' if we could block him from leaving, if he tried to come out by the path of the avalanche. If we'd stay just on this side of the crest, he'd never see us, and we're betting he's terrified of Slobbers and Drool. Especially the two of them together. They can show their faces every now and then and make him think about it. Especially because he didn't hit them when he shot at them. They're kinda like ghost dogs."

"We're hoping he doesn't have another gun," Bud adds. "And we were thinkin' maybe Timber and his pack could block him from leavin' by the old Wildlands service road. We looked at the maps, and those are the only two ways in and out."

Boy oh boy, another adventure for Drool and me?

I look at him; he looks at me and nods. Ghost dogs? That sounds so cool! We're definitely up to it. We're makin' a dent in Cole's floor with all our tail thumpin'.

"It could work," Cole muses. "I'll have to find Timber and have the boys talk to him." He nods at us.

"We should be able to find them with the drone. With the new camera, we should be able to spot tracks or disturbed snow because there's still snow up there," Bud says.

"I think this could work." Cole grins.

"Quite a plan, isn't it?" Dad smiles. "These kids."

"We're here," Darius says, "to flesh it out.

"Have you talked to the Wildlands rangers?" Cole asks. "Is there anything they can do?"

"Good news there," Darius says. "They can pick him up for trespassing in the shack. He needs a permit to be there, and he doesn't have one. Also for snowmobiling in an out-of-bounds area, triggering an avalanche, and on suspicion of attempting to illegally trap wolves. They have to get the okay from headquarters, which they're working on."

"How long will that take?" Cole asks.

"Maybe a week, maybe more. Red tape you know," Darius frowns. "Though Jamie promised to push it."

"Okay," Liu has been quiet to this point. "Let's have the kids see if they can track down an address or at least a 'last known' for this Seth fellow. Then we'll know if he actually has someplace else to go, or if he's hanging out at that line shack because he doesn't. Maybe he's a fugitive again. I can join Cole in the afternoons, and I'm thinking we don't need to worry about after dark. Trying to get out either way is treacherous."

~

Bro and I are getting stiff necks from watching the drone zoom in and out of sight and up and down. Cole and the boys are watching the monitor and the shack right in the middle of it. The snowmobile is there. *Whoopee!*

When Cole sees some trampled snow, he moves the drone lower then looks at Bro and me. We head toward the area with great leaps and bounds, taking a few minutes to roll around in the snow before we get down to business. We might as well have some fun while we're up here!

Now, though, it's all business. The big guy appears. We *oof* and *arf* what the men want done. Is that a smile or a snarl Timber shows us?

Actually, it's both. Yes, his pack will do it, and he's making clear what he thinks of the man. With that, we bound our way back through the snow. Romping and rolling to taunt the guy in the shack if he's there. Just having a good time if he isn't.

“Good job,” Cole says, giving us each one of his mom’s treats.

~

Cole and I have been at the crest of the ridge for most of the day because we don’t mind coming here on foot. Liu arrives by snowmobile with a

very forlorn Drool hunkered down in front of him, his eyes wide and drool flowing from his jowls. I look at Liu with raised eyebrows. *Arrrror?*

"It's quicker," Liu says with a laugh, seeing the expression on my face. "Don't let him fool you. He loves it!"

Drool's eyes meet mine. *Grufff,* he mutters, assuring me what I'm thinking is right; he hates it! *I'm pretty sure I'd hate it too!*

Cole is laughing, too. Huh. Humans. Sometimes! We have our pride ya know. "Okay, you two, off you go. See if there's anything new."

Happily, we climb over the crest and roll down the slope a ways. We romp and roll around, barking our heads off and making a pretty good scene. This is so much fun, it's hard to believe it's dangerous.

At least Cole says it is. I guess being shot at makes it true. We watch the drone make a pass and return. Howling with great abandon as we go, we rejoin them.

"The snowmobile is still there," Liu tells Cole.

"Do you think he has a phone?" Cole asks.

They both look toward the sky. Cole takes out his binoculars and scans the skyline. "There's a tower to the west on the highest peak," he tells Liu. "Could that be a relay of some sort?"

Liu takes the binoculars and looks. "That's a cell tower." He takes out his phone and turns it on. "The signal strength here is pretty darn strong. I'm betting it is where he is, too. There's nothing to block it, but he's still stuck if Timber is on the job."

"He is," Cole assures him, "and unlike us, he and his pack are there twenty-four seven."

Dark is beginning to fall, so we decide to call it a day. Liu wants to go while it's still light enough to see. Cole and I enjoy walking. We know all the shortcuts, and what and where to avoid.

"Liu?" Cole asks as Liu is boosting Bro onto the seat. "I tried calling my mom a few times, but she doesn't answer. Am I doing something wrong with this gadget?"

"Ah!" Liu says, "I'll bet no one told you, what with all this going on. Molly is working at the gallery. At least for the Christmas season."

"She is?" Cole looks surprised.

"Yep. She told the girls about her art background on one of their visits. I've been busy with this, leaving Lian to handle both the office and the gallery, so we asked your mom if she'd like a part-time job."

"You did? My gosh!" Cole is stammering. "How great! Is she doing okay? She had to give up her art ambitions after she married my...father... and they moved here. Because I came along. I always hoped she'd be able to get back to it. She's quite talented, you know."

Bro is situated, looking miserable again, as Liu swings his leg over his share of the seat. "I do know," he grins at Cole. "She's shown us some of her work, and we're thinking we may do a show for her sometime next summer. For now, however, she is one heck of a saleslady and a real asset to the gallery."

Cole is staring at Liu, his mouth open. "How in the world do I ever rate having friends like you?"

Liu starts the engine. "Because you're one of the good guys," he says with a grin. "See you tomorrow!"

~

Cole and I are at our post every day. The snow has held off, which has made sitting around okay. Cole lets me go over the crest several times just in case our culprit is looking in our direction, though I'm not so sure I look very big from as far away as we are. Every afternoon Liu joins us for a couple of hours. Bro always arrives in his place on the seat and has taken to looking like the noble beast he is. I think he's beginning to enjoy it! When we do our romp, I really tease him about it though. *Big strong Saint Bernard being wheeled around!*

Darius finally brings good news. The Wildlands higher-ups have given the go-ahead to pick up our man. I'm glad. It's getting really boring even with the kids and all the men with us again.

"Good!" Cole exclaims. "When? We've got to call off Timber."

"Today! This afternoon!" Darius seems concerned. "Do we have enough time?"

Cole looks at Bro and me. We'll do it. We head over the crest and hurtle down the hill full tilt. I'm relishing the exercise after all the sitting around. There has been no new snow the entire time we've been watching, so what tracks there are haven't been covered. Suddenly the fur on the back of my neck bristles. I sense something isn't quite right. Bro looks at me. He senses it, too.

We stop, still a distance from the shack, and listen. The sound we're hearing isn't snowmobiles. It's a funny schlapping sound. Schlap, schlap, schlap. It's getting closer. We look up at the sky and see what looks like a funny, giant drone coming across the treetops behind the shack. I've seen those! On television! They call them choppers, I think. I guess the schlapping sound could be a chopping sound. Maybe they should be called schlappers.

The guy comes running out of the shack. *Oh, no, he's not going to get away on our watch!* Bro and I race toward him.

Then we hear more schlapping sounds. We look up again, and there's another chopper! The man we're after seems confused and freezes in his tracks. He sees us and starts motioning to one of the choppers, like he's telling it to land. The second one gets within feet of the first one. Nose to nose, almost nudging each other. *Wow! Why are there two of them? What's happening?*

Bro and I are close enough to the guy to leap on him if we have to. Bro edges to one side; I go to the other. We're both snarling, teeth bared.

Out of the corner of my eye I see Timber and a couple of his wolves coming up from behind.

There's a sound coming from one of the choppers. It sounds like very loud voices. We can't make out what they're saying, but we all stand our ground. Our man finally realizes the wolves are behind him and screams at one of the choppers. A door slides open, and a man throws out what looks like a rope with slats. For climbing maybe? Right. Like the rope ladders the kids had in the woods.

The second chopper backs off to land; our man runs toward the dangling ladder and grabs on. Timber is closest to him. With a mighty leap he grabs the seat of the man's pants and falls back to the ground. Bro grabs one of his legs at knee height, and I grab the opposite ankle. He's not going anywhere. All three of us are dug in. The chopper tries to go up, its engine whining from the effort, but with all three of us hanging onto the man, who's none too small himself, it can't.

Timber digs in all four of his feet and, with a mighty tug, pulls the man off the ladder. We all tumble into the snow.

Oh no! A man from the other chopper is running toward us with a gun. Bro sits on our man, and I move between the man with the gun and Timber.

He doesn't point it at us! He points the gun at the chopper, motioning for it to land.

Two other men join him. They all have guns. I turn and look at Timber, nodding. He and his sidekicks quietly slip away. I join Bro, still snarling so our prisoner doesn't get any ideas about trying to escape. The men with the guns see we have our man under snarl and paw, and approach the other chopper and motion for the men inside to shut it down and get out.

Cole, Bud, and Deon are racing down the hill, the men right behind.

Dad and Darius approach the men with the guns who are handcuffing the men from the other chopper. They talk. I'm realizing how much I've learned from watching TV with the kids. I'm guessing the guys from the second chopper are the ones from Wildlands Darius was expecting. *Wow! What timing!*

Cole comes running to us. Bro is happily squashing our guy, wagging his tail, and throwing snow in the man's face.

"Nice job!" Cole hugs me and scratches Bro's ears. He has no intention of letting the guy up until the good guys come.

"Okay, Drool," Cole says. He comes for his hug.

The man doesn't move an inch. I wish Timber was still here. He'd be enjoying this, but I'm sure he's just out of sight watching.

"Cole!" The kids race toward us, brimming with excitement. "Our dogs are awesome! Did you catch that action?"

A Wildlands ranger joins us. "Cole? Is that your name?"

Cole nods. "Jamie Holsom," he says, extending his hand. Cole takes off his mitten and shakes it, then the ranger pats each of us on the head. "Your two dogs are really something," he grins. "Along with your buddy, who left."

He goes to the man lying in the snow, prods him with his toe none too gently, rolls him over and forces him to his knees.

"Don't… don't let those wild beasts get me," the man whimpers. "They're crazy! They're probably rabid! I was told giant beasts live in these parts! I didn't believe it! Help me. Please don't let them at me."

I twitch a muscle and growl at him. *Grrrrrr.* Slobber is dripping from my gums and lips. I shake my head letting it fly. *Rabid? I'll show you rabid!*

"See? See?" He's still whimpering, fear written all over his face. "Look at the size of that one! He's a monster." He looks at Cole. "Him, too!" His eyes widen even wider. "He's a monster, too!"

He squints his eyes and looks closely at Cole. Is that a flicker of recognition?

"Wha...Wha...what did you call him?" All the color drains from his face.

"His name is Cole," the ranger says, cuffing the man's hands behind him while telling him his rights now that he's under arrest. The man stares at Cole, his face twisted with fear.

The men join us. We look at Cole, whose face is absolutely blank as he stares back at the man.

"You okay?" Liu touches his arm.

Cole slowly turns away from Seth Craven and looks at Liu. "I don't know," he says quietly. "I really don't know." He motions to me. I nod

to Bro. We'll help him through this; we promise each other.

Then I nuzzle Cole's hand. He puts his hand on my head, patting it. We go back to and beyond the crest of the ridge.

~

We're all quiet as we gather in the cave.

Cole sits in his chair staring into the fire.

He looks up at everyone. “How am I supposed to feel?” he asks. “How am I supposed to feel?”

Dad pulls up the footstool and sits down. “Maybe,” he says softly, “once you get your head around what’s just happened, you’ll feel pretty darned good.”

I lean my head against Cole’s leg, letting the weight of it warm and comfort him.

“We’ll get the other guy, too,” Darius promises, pulling up the chair from the table. “When we do, everything will have come full circle for you.”

Cole looks at him, “Not everything.”

“We want to see these men brought to justice as much as you do. You’ve become like family to all of us,” Liu adds, “and families take care of one another.”

Bud sits on the arm of Cole’s chair, puts an arm around his shoulders, and presses their faces together. “I love you, Cole. You’re like a brother to me.”

"To me, too," Deon says. "We want you to be as happy we've come into your life as we are that you've come into ours."

"I...I guess I'm sort of numb," Cole says. "Seeing him face to face. And that he seemed to remember me, or at least my name, after all these years. What does he feel? Guilt? Somehow I doubt it."

"Terror," Liu suggests. "Pure terror. You're not dead but alive and well. I think perhaps his greatest fear is what you might do."

"What *can* I do?" Cole murmurs. "There's no way to undo any of the evil he's done. Not just to me, but what he did to Timber and who knows how many other animals, and the kids he's hurt with his drug stuff. And adults, too, for that matter. There's no way. Maybe that's why I feel no satisfaction. I just feel empty."

"Would you like one of us to stay with you tonight?"" Dad asks softly.

"Thanks," Cole says, looking at him, "but no. I'm okay. After having survived all these years,

I have no intention of doing anything stupid just because I came face to face with pure evil. I just want to see him get his due and have it stick, once and for all. I guess I just never really expected it to happen. Certainly not the way it did today, thanks to some really smart kids, their fantastic families, and the two best dogs in the world."

BRO

People are strange creatures compared to dogs. We just live our lives from day to day, trying to make our people happy.

People, on the other hand, seem to celebrate everything that comes to mind. We just finished up with Thanksgiving, and, from what I understand, the biggest, most glitzy celebration of all is just a few weeks away. Heck, just since I've been alive there have been five really big ones and a whole bunch more small ones. Small if you think Mother's Day and Father's Day are small! Some are pretty much just for the family; others have parades and fireworks and all kinds of neat stuff.

Ya know what? I haven't heard of one that is Saint Bernard's Day or Love Your Dog Day. There were dog days late last summer, but they were hardly anything to celebrate—unless you consider days so hot not even a dripping tongue or upturned paw pads could relieve the heat as something to celebrate. Cole and Slobbers do it right. They both just go day to day, keeping each other happy. *What more do ya' need?*

~

Now. Comes. Christmas. It's all I'm hearing. Sis and Lin are having their afternoon hot chocolate with Mrs. Black when Sis asks, "Do you and Mr. Black celebrate Christmas?"

"Why, no, no we don't," she says wistfully. "We used to have wonderful Christmases when Cole was with us, but when he left, so did the holiday spirit. We don't even decorate anymore, even though everything is stored in the basement. Wonderful old ornaments and the train Cole loved to set up under the tree."

"How cool!" Sis squeals, "Could we see them sometime?"

"We don't want to stir up bad memories." Lin adds. "Maybe they could be good ones."

"It would be fun," Mrs. Black muses, scratching my ears, "seeing all those things again. Next time you come, we'll have an adventure trying to unearth everything."

Rurrruuf?

"Of course you can come, Drool," she says, laughing. "You can dust things off with your tail."

~

I've never been in a basement before. I wonder if they are all like the Blacks'. As I pick my way down the steps after the girls, I see piles and piles of boxes stacked from the floor to the ceiling. Wispy looking stuff dangles from beams and pipes, draping the tops and sides of boxes that are covered in dust. Everything smells funny, too. How are we going to find anything? There's nothing here that looks like the lights and the other stuff people are putting up outside.

"It may take the four of us to unearth some of these things." Mrs. Black is standing with her hands on her hips. "What a mess! I'm ashamed for you girls to see this."

Hey. She included me. That's pretty cool.

"No worries," Lin says with a giggle, "it looks like Sis's room."

They all laugh. It's true though. Only Sis's room isn't quite so dusty.

I look around to see where I can help. A whoosh of my tail here and a swish there, and huge puffs of dust rise and suddenly the tops of the boxes appear. Ha. This is kind a fun.

Oops. My tail goes swoosh and another cloud of dust nearly swallows all of us. *AAAAAchoooo! Aaaaachooo! AAAACHOOOOH!*

Whew! I blow a whole lot of dust off of all the boxes next to me.

"Look," Sis exclaims, "here's a box marked trains!"

They all scramble to get it where they can open it while I try to stifle some more sneezes.

"Wow!" Lin gasps with delight. "The guys would love this!"

More boxes are opened and more things carefully unwrapped and admired. I've never seen a "train" before. It's a bunch of tiny cars that all hook together and are pulled by an "engine." People sure have a lot of ways to get around. We dogs use our legs unless a human takes us somewhere in a car. Or, like Mr. Huang, on a snowmobile. Mrs. Black seems happy and sad all at the same time, but the girls are having a fine time and I'm not even minding their giggles. It's fun seeing everyone happy and a little silly.

Each piece is rewrapped and placed back in a box. "How wonderful," Lin says. "Maybe we could put the train around the tree in the gallery?"

"And use some of the ornaments too," Sis suggests.

"Mom and Dad would love it. They are so beautiful; they should be shared and enjoyed instead of boxed away," Lin says. "Could we, Mrs. Black?"

"We'll ask," she agrees. "It would be wonderful for others to be able to see some of these treasures. Not many people do this type of craftsmanship anymore."

Sis and Lin signal each other with their now familiar thumbs-up as they head for the steps behind Mrs. Black. I start to step over a box, slip on a paper bag full of old newspapers, sneeze again, and fall flat on my face. The newspapers burst into the air, then drift back to the floor all around me.

Rooorr, I apologize.

Sis and Lin laugh and step over me to pick them up.

"Wow, what's this?" Sis holds up a page for Lin and Mrs. Black to see. It shows a picture of a young man holding a dead wolf in one hand and a bunch of traps in the other. He is smirking like he's proud of himself. I bristle. I can't look at it.

Mrs. Black gasps and starts looking through more of the papers.

"They all look like the same guy!" Lin exclaims.

"But the papers are all from different towns," Sis observes. "This is creepy."

Mrs. Black picks up a brown envelope from the floor. It's filled with smaller pieces of paper with writing on them. She picks a page and begins to read. She sinks to a step, her hand covering her mouth. She suddenly looks very pale.

Sis takes it from her, reads it, and hands it to Lin.

"Oh, my." Mrs. Black begins to weep. "Oh my, oh my, oh my."

"These papers and letters are really old," Lin says quietly. "Look how yellow they are. Had you forgotten about them?"

Mrs. Black looks up at her. “I never knew about them.”

“Does Mr. Black know about them?” Lin asks.

“He must. Who else could? Why wouldn’t he tell me? Why wouldn’t he tell me?”

Sis and Lin look at each other.

“Mrs. Black,” Sis says, “how did you find out Cole was alive after everyone else thought he was dead? Why would anyone think he was still alive after a year?"

"He...he left me a note," Mrs. Black says, her face pale, "where he knew I'd find it. Where I have the spare key to my car. I always, always checked to make sure it was there because I have a bad habit of setting my keys down and forgetting where. Under the front fender. We started exchanging notes, and things just went on from there. Why?"

"It seems like someone wondered if he was really dead after all that time. Do you know who this guy is?" Sis asks.

Mrs. Black studies the photos and shakes her head no. "I can't be sure," she says, "the creases hide a lot of his features."

"But not that snarly grin," Lin says. "Mrs. Black, would you let us borrow some of these? I'm thinking there might be a connection between the wolf poacher the guys just caught and this guy. We can scan them into my computer and see if there's a match or enough of one that maybe we should tell our parents."

"A computer can do that?" Mrs. Black cries. "What does all this mean? I wouldn't know where to begin. Do you think you can help figure it out?

"I think so," Sis takes her hand. "Plus, we know our parents will help."

I'm not sure what is happening, but my senses tell me it isn't good. I nuzzle Mrs. Black's hand, and she gives me a huge hug, burying her face in my ruff. "It's horrible. It's just horrible!"

~

The ladies are hovering around Mrs. Black oohing and aahing over the boxes as the girls and I come clomping into the gallery, stomping snow off our feet.

"Thank heavens you're all here," Sis says excitedly.

"You're white as a sheet," Mom exclaims, "what's wrong?"

"We have something you need to see," Lin says. "When we were looking for Christmas stuff with Mrs. Black, we found these old papers and letters..." Sis hands each of the women a paper and a letter. After reading through them, they look at Mrs. Black in horror.

"I didn't even know these existed." She comes to me and scratches my ears, "Until Drool found an old paper bag full of them. As you can see, whoever they are suspected Cole was still alive, but it would be better for him and us if he stayed dead."

The women gasp.

"The girls thought they could do some sleuthing like the men and boys did with the wolf poacher to figure out who this is and why he'd threaten us."

"I remembered I have a facial recognition app on my computer," Lin says, "so we scanned the best of the photos and ran them through to see if there was a match. We really got lucky because there was a photo of our wolf poacher in a database, and we got a match!"

"There's a glitch though," Sis chimes in. "Not all the photos are of the same guy, and we don't have a clue as to who the other one is. They

used all different names and ran it in a bunch of different papers. Or pretended to. They were Photoshopped."

"What's Photoshopped?" Mrs. Black asks.

"Altered, faked," Mrs. Brown says. "It would appear they did all this to instill fear in the Blacks? But why? Why would they have thought Cole was alive? And why would it matter to them if he was?"

Mrs. Huang asks, "Is it possible these young men are the boys who dosed Cole?"

"That's easy enough to find out," Lin says. "All we need to do is scan pictures from their high school yearbooks and see if they match."

Wow. I am so impressed with these girls. They may not have built a drone but they sure know computers!

"I tried and tried to get Pitch to talk with the authorities about Cole's side of the story, but he absolutely refused to hear any of it. I couldn't understand his attitude. He loved Cole. If only he'd told me about these threats, we could have defended our son, but he wanted him gone. Now I'm thinking that wasn't the case at all! Maybe Pitch did believe Cole," she says, tears streaming down her face, "and forced him leave to protect him."

"Do you think he knows Cole is alive?" Mom asks.

"I don't think so," Mrs. Black picks up the toy train engine and turns it over and over in her hands. "When the authorities told us they were closing the case he picked up and left. He stayed away for a couple of months, never sending me one word of where he had gone or when he'd be back. If he'd be back. He came back a totally different man. We stayed together because I had nowhere to go, and no skills. What I did have was the knowledge that Cole was indeed alive, though to this day I've not seen him."

"Unfortunately," Mom says, looking grim, "someone else has."

~

The kids decide Cole needs to see the papers, fearing for his safety.

"What's up, kids?" He greets us as we all burst out of the meadow.

"You need to see these," Sis says, wheezing from the run. "Do you know this guy? We found a whole bag full of this stuff in your mom's basement."

We gather around Cole's table and watch him spread the papers. Slobbers gives me a "what the heck is going on" look, and I give him a "just listen" look in return.

Cole gets the scrapbook in which he keeps the cloth swatches. "I'd say it's the same guys," he says quietly. "Wouldn't you?"

They all stare at the photos, nodding.

"Deon, give your dad a call and see if our Mr. Craven is still in jail."

He comes back to where we're waiting. "Dad says he is. His bail hearing is the day after tomorrow."

Cole nods. "We need to make sure he doesn't get bail. I'm hoping against hope the guys from Wildlands can give a good argument against it. But if someone offers to post it, we need to know who that person is. Do you guys think you're up to the task?"

Of course, we are! I can answer for them for sure. *Rrrrr, rrrrrr.*

I go whine at the door. Deon opens it for both Slobbers and me. Once outside, I paw and snort around describing what has happened. We decide we need Timber's help again and send up a howl. Within minutes, he's on the ridge of rocks above the cave, one eyebrow cocked, asking what has happened.

Not to worry, he assures Slobbers and myself. His pack will make sure no harm comes to Cole or to Slobbers.

The kids join us for the walk home. Cole looks up and sees Timber watching us, gives him a small salute, and then he and Slobbers watch as Timber goes off to do what it is he does.

~

"Hey guys," Sis breaks the silence in what has been a long, quiet walk. "I've got an idea. On how to track someone if they try to make bail for that guy." Everyone turns their attention to her. "I was gonna do this for Christmas for Slobbers and Drool. They make these remotes you put on your dog's collar so you can use an app on your phone to keep track of where they are.

"Why don't we put one on a magnet," she says, explaining about Mrs. Black's safe place for her car keys, "and when we know whose car it is, stick one on it. Then we can track it."

"Sis," Bud says with a grin, "sometimes you amaze me! It just might work."

"But we can't go to the hearing, can we?" Lin asks.

"Dad says it's scheduled for four. We'll be outta school by then. We can just hang out outside the courthouse."

"Like four kids and a big dog won't be obvious," Lin says.

"What about the guy from Wildlands who was talking to Cole?" Deon suggests. "Maybe he would help. His name should be in the story about the arrest."

"I thought I had it with me." Sis looks through the papers she still has. "Where the heck is it?"

We take off full tilt for Lin's house, which is closest. The kids rummage through the Huang's stash of old newspapers set aside for recycling.

"Here it is," Lin squeals her excitement. "His name is Ranger Jamie Holsom."

"Fantastic. We'll meet at school and head straight to the Wildlands office. Bring the papers and letters. We'll get Mom to take Drool to the gallery, and we can pick him up there."

"What if this Jamie isn't there?" Sis asks.

"He'll be there," Lin says with determination. "He has to be."

"Bud, why don't you call him from school to make sure he'll be there," Deon suggests. "He seemed like a pretty cool guy. Did you notice he never gave Cole's size, or Slobbers, a second glance?"

"That could be good or bad" Sis says. "What if he's one of them?"

"Man," Deon groans.

SLOBBERS

Cole hasn't stopped pacing since the kids left. I feel helpless. I sense we could be in danger, but nothing has me on edge right now. Of course, it helps that Timber has our backs.

"I've gotta do something," Cole says. "My whole family could be in danger!"

I nose around the papers strewn on the floor and come across a recent one that has the story about Seth Craven's arrest. Where did that come from? One of the kids must have dropped it. It doesn't matter. It could be important, so I paw at it until I get Cole's attention.

"What's this?" He picks it up and reads it. "That's it! Ranger Holsom. We've got to get to him!"

We stay in the trees just away from the part of the ranger station where the men stay when they're on duty. Cole wraps a note around my collar and motions for me to go to the door. I scratch at it.

Nothing. I bark. That should get their attention! The door opens just a crack.

"What the..." a voice from inside says.

"What is it?" Another voice says, and then a face appears. "Well. Hi there, big guy! What brings you here?"

I scratch at the note. He sees it, takes it from me, and reads it.

"It's okay," he calls over his shoulder as he grabs a jacket. "I'll be right back."

Cole is sitting on a rock as we get to him, trying, I think, not to look so tall.

"Cole," the man says, "this is a surprise. What's happening?"

Cole spills the whole story to the young man, who doesn't appear to be all that much older than Cole.

"Wow," Jamie Holsom exhales. "That's quite a story. We've been after these guys for a very long time, and I've become very aware that someone has been lending us a hand. I'm assuming that would be you, this fine fellow, and the leader of this region's resident wolf pack."

Cole nods.

"I don't know if I can help you with the doping, but I sure as heck can with the poaching, the trespassing, and the triggering of the avalanche! Do you want to come to the hearing?"

"No! No. I don't want to do anything to further endanger my family. But do me a favor. If you get a call before the hearing from a youngster named Bud, Deon, Lin, or Sis or their families, please hear them out. They're my eyes, ears, and lifeline."

The men exchange phone numbers. Jamie cements his friendship with me by giving me a huge hug and ear scratch. I return the favor with as dry a kiss as I can manage.

"I'll be in touch," Jamie says. "Stay cool. Or try to. I have a lot I'd like to talk to you about."

Cole nods, raises himself to his full height, and the men shake hands. "Ever play basketball?" Jamie asks. "We could use a center on the bureau's team!"

BRO

We meet Ranger Jamie Holsom behind the courthouse, where we can't be seen.

"I have a plan," he says as we all listen eagerly. "Someone who knows Craven, besides his lawyer, will be in that courtroom, I'm sure. He's a loose cannon and probably has his higher-ups worried. Someone will be here to report to them. My guess is they'll come in a pretty ordinary looking rental car because they won't want to draw attention to themselves. Do you know what rental car stickers look like?" He explains to the kids where and what to look for.

"So, here's what I think we should do. I'll be out really fast if bail is denied because Mr. Big or his rep will be wanting to split. If bail is granted, it may take a little longer because there are procedures to be followed. I'm trusting you kids to find the car, and get the make, description, license number, and the rental company. My guess is they'll head to the airport either way, and the authorities will be able to give us the info we need on their plane—which will be a private one."

"We have a plan," Bud assures Jamie.

~

The only ones on the street are the kids and me. I stick close to the girls as we roam among the cars looking for rental stickers. We are lucky. There is only one. There is also a shady-looking guy leaning against it, smoking. He's a bad one. I know. I sense it.

Bud motions us to gather where we can't be seen. "That's gotta be the car," he whispers.

"Yeah," Deon agrees, "he must be the designated stooge who has to turn it in to the rental agent."

"Then where will he go?" Lin asks.

The boys shrug.

"That's no answer," Sis hisses, "we've got to get a remote on him, too. So we know where he goes. He's one of them!"

"But how?" Deon asks.

"Well," Sis says, "I have two of them. We can stick one on the car like we planned, and Lin

and I will have to stick the other one in his jacket pocket."

"Oh, boy," Deon says. "That could be dangerous!"

"We'll handle it," Sis assures them, "with Drool's help."

Man, I love these challenges! You know, I'm gaining a lot of respect for the gigglers.

People are beginning to come out of the courthouse, and Jamie is right in front. That's good news. The guy didn't get bail.

The girls move in front of the rental car. I'm hovering behind them ready to leap at the guy if necessary. I'm aching for the chance. I'm getting' pretty tired of bad guys.

"You always think you know everything!" Sis screams at Lin.

"You little twit," Lin yells back, "you think you're something special because you have that big dumb dog!"

Big dumb dog? Whoa! Oops. I forget for a second how good they are at drama!

The girls begin hitting each other, actually pummeling each other, pulling each other's hair, screaming at each other at the top of their lungs, and nearly wrestling each other to the ground. Man, I knew these two were good at drama, but they're really outdoing themselves here!

Woof, WOOF! I'm barking frantically, trying to keep them from actually hurting each other as I see the boys have succeeded in placing one remote under the car.

The man who had been leaning against the car tries to get between the girls. "Break it up," he snarls, grabbing Lin's arm. "You're making too much of a commotion!"

"LET GO OF ME YOU CREEP! STRANGER DANGER! STRANGER DANGER!" She's really screaming now, and people are stopping to look. *Wow, this kid has a voice!*

Sis leaps on the guy, flailing at him with all her might. "LEAVE MY FRIEND ALONE! HOW DARE YOU! WHO DO YOU THINK YOU ARE?"

Man, this is getting dicey! I move in close to the guy who has hold of Lin, growling loudly, just in case he forgot I'm here. So far, though, she's holding her own, hitting just as hard as Sis. He's gonna have some serious bruises! I'll tell ya, Lin and Sis are every bit as brave as Bud and Deon! In this case, maybe even more!

Yippee! Sis slips the remote into his pocket. Jamie races in and grabs the man, wrestling him away from Lin and keeping an eye on two men climbing into the car.

"Let go of the girl, or I'll have to arrest you." His voice is menacing.

"I'm outta here," the guy sneers, taking a kick at me. *Grrrrrr.* This time, I give him a bare-toothed snarl.

I leap at him just as he slams the door closed.

"Drool, are you okay?" Sis cries.

Woof. I assure her I am. Just angry. And relieved the girls are safe.

I stand between the girls and the car as it roars away. Jamie calms the onlookers. He winks at the girls and gives a thumbs-up to the boys. I think maybe I'm the only one who sees Seth Craven leaving the courthouse tightly secured between two police officers.

Man, I need to learn how to give a thumbs up, too. A satisfied *arf* will have to do.

SLOBBERS

I hear the footsteps before the knock. Cole and I look at each other. It's a strange time of day for anyone to be visiting. The kids should be in school and everyone else at work. I'm ready to pounce as Cole cracks the door.

"Jamie! What are you doing here? How did you find us?"

"The kids didn't think you'd mind, so they told me," he holds out a small pine tree that is covered with shiny, bright balls and shapes with a star on top.

"What's this?"

"This is a Christmas tree," Jamie laughs, "in case you've forgotten. Everyone thought you and Slobbers should have one."

Cole shakes his head, taking it and setting it on the table.

"You've got yourself quite a fan club, you know?"

COLE

"Totally undeserved but awfully darned nice. So, what happened? Is everyone okay? Is my mom okay? It was killing me not to be there."

"That was your choice," Jamie says. "I'm hoping your friends will accept me and my men into this fan club of yours, and between all of us we can get you out of here."

"Easier said than done." Cole hands Jamie a cup of tea.

"Ooooo, nice. Home brew?"

Cole nods.

Jamie laughs, shaking his head. "My man, you have no idea what all you have to offer the outside world if only you'd rejoin it."

Arrrorrrrrr. I agree.

"To answer your question, your mom is fine and so is your dad. Seth Craven was denied bail, and he is being held at the county jail over in Calamity. There will be a hearing on pending charges after the first of the year. In the meantime, he isn't going anywhere. Zip. Zero. Zilch.

He's a flight risk and a danger to the community. No bail under any circumstances.

"The men who had hoped to get him out had a private plane waiting, but we got all the info on the charter to expand the investigation. The question is where in the organization are they? Near the top? Middle? Bottom? Craven," he says with a laugh, "is rock bottom. Or maybe a smidgen above the guy who was arrested in Serenity this summer. Craven was his handler.

"The guy who drove the rental car took a cab to the bus station and bought a ticket for Metroburg. We notified authorities to see if they can track him once he gets there. My guess, however, is he's probably on Craven's level. Not good for much other than doing dirty work."

"Wow," Cole exclaims, "how did you ever manage to track them?"

"Two young ladies who have a huge crush on you came up with a fantastic scheme," Jamie says, laughing. "Drool played a pretty significant role too."

The girls? Lin and Sis? Bro? Wow. I sure wish I had been there. Well, of course Drool would play a significant role. After all, he's my twin brother!

"Well, my friend," Jamie sets his cup down, "duty calls. Give me a call if you feel like talking." He goes to the tree and sets an envelope down next to it.

"What's that?"

Jamie shrugs. "It's for you."

Cole sees Jamie out, then picks up the envelope. He turns it over a couple of times before he opens it.

Arrorr?

"Dear Cole," he reads, "You and Slobbers are hereby invited to the Christmas celebration held annually by the Browns, the Huangs, and the Whites. Festivities this year will be at the Whites and will begin at noon Christmas day. Dinner will be served at three p.m. sharp. Please come. The good guys." He slumps into his chair. "You know, Slobbers, I almost wish we could go."

Arrrrgggg. We can and you know it.

~

Christmas is two days away, so Cole tells me. No one has been to see us even though there really isn't enough snow to keep them away. I guess they're busy getting ready for whatever Christmas is.

There is a knock. I was wondering if we'd been forgotten, but maybe not.

"Liu?" Mr. Huang is standing at the door, his arms filled with packages.

"May I come in?" he grins.

"Of course, of course. What's all this?"

Liu drops the packages on the table. "This," he says in a very serious voice, "is from Santa, and today I am his designated elf."

Cole watches as Liu spreads all the packages out, then chooses a very small one and opens it.

"Shave and a haircut, free of charge," he says, smiling and holding a comb, a razor, and scissors. "If you trust me to have a steady hand."

"Wha...what?"

"Next," he opens a much larger package, "let's see if my artistic eye has guessed your proportions correctly." He shakes out what the kids call underwear. Shorts, shirts, socks, that kind of stuff.

"This was a tough one," he says, opening a couple of boxes of brand new shoes. "But guaranteed to be comfortable the first time you wear them."

Next he picks up a long bag with a zipper, which he unzips.

"Perfectly pressed," he says, "and ready to wear." It holds shirts, pants, sweaters and even a coat! "Now, shall we try that shave and a haircut?"

Cole is shaking his head. I'm enjoying the show thoroughly. Liu has always been a really fun guy, and this is no exception. He snips and combs and snips some more, checking his work from every angle.

When he's done, he whips out a mirror. "You know, you're not a bad looking dude underneath all that scruff."

Both men are in the spirit of the moment. Cole tries on his new clothes as Liu showers him with

compliments. He even plops a funny red hat with white trim and a small white ball on the tip of it on my head! He holds the mirror so I can see. *Silly. Snaaaaarf. Kinda nice to be included though.*

They're laughing as they talk and they talk about Mrs. Black and her talent, the kids and what heroes they are, and how Drool fits right into the gang. Just like me. That's so great to hear! They talk like they're the best of friends, and in many ways they are. I am so happy and proud to be part of all of it and even happier that Bro... Drool...is now sharing all of it with me.

Liu finally has to leave. He sees the envelope next to the Christmas tree and taps it.

"See you soon," he says with a grin, heading out the door.

Cole stands in the middle of all his new things, scratching his head. He picks up the mirror and studies his face again, turning his head from side to side.

"Now what do I do?" he asks me. "I know they're all friends, but, like I have nothing to give them. It's Christmas, Slobbers. I guess you don't know anything about it since this is your first one. Everyone exchanges presents." He waves his hand at everything laying around him.

"What can I possible give?"

Yoooooorrroo, I murmur quietly. Your presence. He looks at me for a time, then shakes his head again.

"I can't, Slobbers; I just can't. Too many people. I'll panic. I'll make a fool of myself."

You can too do it, I want to shout. Look how far you've come, thanks to these people. How can you *not* go! Perplexed I begin nosing through the wrappings that are strewn about, then I have a bright idea. *A brilliant idea!* I go to the boxes and boxes of books he has stacked all over the place.

"Arrorrr?" I paw at them, even knocking them over so he has to pick them up. He looks at me. Suddenly a huge grin crosses his face.

"Are you sure you're just a dog?" He's laughing. "You're wonderful, brave, smart, savvy, and even know how to talk! What would I ever have done without you?"

He hugs me so hard, I think I'm going to burst.

BRO

This Christmas thing is really something. For weeks, the village has been decked out in colorful lights and decorated pine trees and wreaths of pine and holly and berries in windows and bells on doors. The people have been going around neighborhoods singing songs, some light-hearted and fun, others quiet and just...just beautiful. Everyone is in a good mood.

Since the arrest of Seth Craven, the kids have been getting along better than ever. They seemed to have gained a mutual respect for each other, even though the boys can be a bit snarky at times and the gigglers over-dramatic. *But hey, they're kids.*

One night, the whole family gathers around the tree in our living room and decorates it. Mom is spending days in the kitchen baking cookies and getting ready for the big dinner that is going to be at our house.

I'm really happy Mrs. Black told Mom she would come, but Mr. Black sent his regrets. *Regrets? C'mon.* If Cole can move on, he can too! Someday, I'm gonna meet that guy. Here he has a wonderful wife and a great son, and all he does is hang out at his pub and make beer. I wonder if he has a clue about what he's missing!

Late on the night before Christmas, the kids go to bed. Mom and Dad have been hiding in the den for a lot of the evening, and now they come out with beautiful packages covered in shimmering paper and fanciful bows. This is a most interesting activity because they just leave them after putting them down. They motion to me, and we go off to bed.

Christmas morning, the family gathers to open the packages! These are presents for each other, Bud explains to me. Others will be exchanged with all our friends later in the day.

I wonder if there's anything in them for me? *Oh, boy, there is! New chew toys!* I'm still a puppy you know! Rawhide bones. Toys that squeak or that have bells in them that jingle. Some real honest-to-gosh meaty bones like Cole always had for me. *Wow! No wonder people like this holiday!*

The house smells wonderful. Coffee. Bacon. Turkey in the oven. Cookies. Pine from the tree. Even the fire in the fireplace has a wonderful scent. Even if I didn't drool, I'd be drooling over all these smells! This is about as festive as I need. It's all a bit overwhelming. I wish Slobbers was here with me to enjoy it. Maybe he'll come later. No one has said anything about him, though.

There's a knock on the door. It's the Browns and the Huangs. They are all loaded down with packages and what seems to be more food! Wow.

Another knock. Mrs. Black with her arms loaded, too. Man, everyone sure chips in for this celebration!

Another knock? It's Jamie Holsom and a very pretty young lady he introduces as his fiancée, Jodie. They, too, come bearing packages of all sorts. *This is going to be some day!* Not that it hasn't been already.

SLOBBERS

Cole spends most of the night going through all his boxes of books. He picks out four and sets them aside. I can tell they mean a great deal to him by the way he holds them and looks at them. He smiles.

He looks around, his gaze stopping on the little tree. Carefully, he takes four balls from it, each a different color, and ties one to each book, then places them in a box. Then he rummages through another box that contains the little carvings he works on and pulls out three different poses of Timber. He really just finished them in the last few days. He wraps each separately with paper that had wrapped some of his new clothes and places them in the box with the books.

Then he turns to me. "Slobbers, c'mon. I want you to see something," he says quietly.

We go outside. The stars are shimmering in the sky. There is no wind; it is absolutely still and silent. The moon is huge and full.

"To me," Cole says softly, "it doesn't get any better than this."

I'm not surprised when I hear the voices of Timber and our friends celebrating that very same moon. Then there he is on top of the rocks, his eyes glowing golden in the night. He looks down at us.

"Merry Christmas to you and yours, Timber!" Cole shouts at the top of his lungs. Timber sits back on his haunches, and, silhouetted against

that moon, raises his head, and howls good wishes in return.

~

Cole disappears for a time into his makeshift shower and comes back clean-shaven and smelling like he's never smelled before. Actually, he smells a lot like Dad does when he heads out to work in the morning. *It's pretty nice, but it sure isn't food!*

He goes to where he's hung up his new clothes and picks out pants and a sweater. He looks pretty darned handsome when he's all dressed. He still wears his old moccasins, but I think maybe he doesn't want to get his new shoes wet. Mom used to yell at the kids when they wore their good shoes in the wet.

He picks up my new red hat and puts it on my head. "Hmmm." He finds a piece of cord, pokes holes on each side of my hat, ties the cord on, and then ties it under my chin. Super. Now it won't fall off. I'd sure hate to lose it, even if it is silly.

"Okay, Slobbers," he says, scratching my ears. "Let's get this show on the road before I lose my nerve!" He tucks the box with the books and carvings along with his new shoebox under his arm, and off we go.

As we get close to the Whites' house, we can hear the voices from inside, the laughter, the singing. What a great time they seem to be having. I wonder if Drool is enjoying all of it! Cole glances at his watch, then stops dead in his tracks.

I almost knock him over.

"I...I'm not sure I can do this..."

I grab his sleeve and give him a mighty jerk. *You can! You absolutely can!*

He looks down at me, lets out a deep sigh, and lowers his head, and we make our way around to the front of the house. *Atta boy Cole!* Sis is looking out the window.

"Mom, Dad, it's Cole and Slobbers," she shouts. "They came; they came; they're coming; they're outside!"

George opens the door and everyone races outside to greet us. The kids are all over Cole and me, tugging and pulling us into the house as he actually tries to change his shoes. It's kinda funny

in a way, and in a way, it tells me how much he really cares.

"Watch your head." Dad laughs. "We've got nine-foot ceilings but not the door!"

Mrs. Black is standing alone by the door to the dining room.

Mom comes up to Cole. "I'm Sarah," she says softly. "You look wonderful." She takes his hand. "Come, say hello to your mother."

Their eyes meet. They stand silent for a moment staring at each other. Then Cole rushes to her, picks her clear off the floor, and swings her around and around, his head buried in her shoulder. Neither says a word.

Tears are streaking both their faces.

Everyone watches quietly. There's not a dry eye in the house.

Bud ends the moment, shouting, "Time for presents!" Drool curls up by Dad; I stay close to Cole as best I can. With so many people moving about and me being so big, it isn't easy, but it's where I sense I need to be.

"All right," Dad says. "We have a very special guest with us today. Mr. Cole Black. So, let's bestow upon him his due."

Cole is looking a bit bewildered as he settles on the couch with his mom clinging to his arm.

"First," Dad continues, "we have newcomer to the gang of good guys, Mr. Jamie Holsom, and, of course, his lovely bride-to-be, Jodie. Jamie?"

"I've not known Cole but for a few weeks," he says, "but I've been aware of the work he's been doing ever since I've been here, which has been about two years. We've needed a director for the Serenity sector for the Bureau of Wildlands for years and could never find anyone who wanted to do the job. Then I realized someone was already doing it. Cole, think it over and we'll talk, but the job is officially yours if you want it. You've been doing it for years and doing it better than we could have asked. It's time you get paid for it."

Cole's mouth drops open. His mom squeezes his arm and the room fills with applause. *Ooooooww-ww, Owoooo!* Drool and I both voice our approval. Dad raises his hand and everyone quiets.

"Okay. I'll admit to some brainstorming with Jamie on this, but from the Browns, the Huangs, and the Whites will come a fully furnished cabin to be placed at your discretion, to serve as home and headquarters—or just home if you don't take the job. The women of our households will decorate and furnish it to suit your taste and lifestyle. It can be right next to the cave if you'd like but we're thinking some errant bear might like that cave!"

Cole's mouth is still ajar. He is totally speechless. Again, everyone claps enthusiastically.

"Lin and Sis?" Dad says.

"We put up a funding site that drew a lot of attention," Sis says.

"Yeah, from just regular people who love dogs and a lot of companies that provide for them one way or another, we've been able to raise enough to provide food and veterinarian care for both Slobbers and Drool for as long as they need it. Mr. White is going to invest it for us to make sure it never runs out, and Jodie has volunteered to be their vet since she'll be working with Wildlands and will be close."

Lin adds, "and for you Slobbers..." They lay out a slew of toys and a giant box of Mrs. Black's special dog treats. They hug me and tell me, "Drool got his this morning!"

Oh man, I sniff and paw at everything with great enthusiasm *arooooooing* my thanks. *For me! Arrrrf, aaaarf!* My tail is working overtime. And a vet? To take care of Drool and me? *How great is that??* I just hope they don't have to get me on a table for an exam!

The girls turn to Cole and give him a big hug. He enfolds them in his arms in return.

"Boys?" Dad calls Bud and Deon front and center. "We were thinking you'd need some help patrolling the sector, so we asked a bunch of our school friends if they'd like to volunteer to be junior rangers of sorts to help you out. Jamie thinks it would be great and has cleared it with headquarters. We're gonna make a formal proposal and everything. The robotics club is stoked, too, 'cause they figure they can try out a whole lot of innovative stuff to help out. Mr. Garcia, our club advisor, is all for it too!"

"Yeah," Deon adds, "most of kids around here are really into the outdoors, but those who aren't still want to be a part of it and will help with the innovating. Even a lot of girls are keen on it. A lot of them would like to help when you have injured animals and stuff like that, too!"

Cole looks from person to person, not able to utter a word. He shakes his head in disbelief. "Wh...Why?" he finally manages.

"Because you're the founder and CEO of the Gang of Good Guys," Liu says with a grin. "This community needs you, and your family needs you; we all need and want you to be one with us."

"But...but look at me," he mumbles.

"What should we see other than a center for Jamie's bureau basketball team?" Darius laughs and everyone joins in.

"Okay, okay," Cole says softly. "I'll try. It may take me some time to get used to all of this. Bud really accelerated things when he brought George out to meet me, but everything that's happened since has been pretty overwhelming."

"Not to worry," Liu says, "we're very patient people."

"And, as a bonus," Darius adds, "we've got a lead on one Damian Price aka so many names I can't begin to remember them, but the lead is solid."

Aaarrrroooo, I let out a reminder to Cole that he has some presents to distribute, too.

"Right," he pats my head. "I can't begin to match what you people have done for me, but I couldn't come empty-handed."

They follow Cole outside and quickly return with the boxes. “What’s this?” Dad asks.

“Kids first.” Cole smiles. “It isn’t much, but I sorted through all my books and picked out ones I think each of you might enjoy. Some are really, really old. They may even be first editions. Mom can help clear that up.”

The kids open their packages and take out the books. There is a chorus of “Oh, wows!” and “This is fantastic!” and other exclamations of surprise and wonder. All four of the kids pile on Cole, giving him hugs and thank you's and love.

Aimee Brown, who is the village librarian, says, "You couldn't have given better gifts than books, Cole." The other adults all nod their agreement. Everyone is looking a bit weepy again.

"The rest is kind of 'couples' gifts," Cole says, handing each couple a small package. "I didn't know what to do. It isn't much." They open their boxes, each holding one of the carved wolves.

"Cole, these are exquisite!" Lian exclaims. "Your mother isn't the only artist in the family!"

Cole looks a little sheepish. Why, I'm not sure. He spent a lot of our free time whittling away on the little pieces. They are beside themselves, totally in awe of his craftsmanship.

"Jamie, I owe you. I didn't know you...and Jodie would be here."

"No matter." Jamie smiles. "Just take the job. That will be the best gift you could give me."

The two young men grin at each other. Yes! I can tell they like each other. As great as the kids are, Cole really needs a friend close to his own age, sorta like the kids need each other. And Drool and I. We all need each other.

Cole turns to his mother. "Mom, I know you played a huge part in making all of this happen. The biggest, actually, by believing in me all these years. Of all the people I should have something for, I don't. I...I'm so sorry," he shrugs, looking helpless, and bows his head.

"You've come back," she says softly, taking his face in her hands and kissing his cheek. "You've come back. You couldn't give me a better gift."

~

Drool and I are watching the festivities as we lay curled against the door and each other. Even with being half on top of one another, it's the coolest place in the house where we can still see everything that's going on. Everyone has been noshing food from the buffet, and Drool and I have been fed tidbits of roast beef and turkey and ham and assorted other goodies I don't know what to call! If we were cats, we'd be purring like well-

tuned engines because we're so proud of the part we've played in bringing all our friends together. Which, if I do say so, has been a lot.

Suddenly Drool bats me with his paw and nods toward the window beside the door.

Parf. Is that a person out there?

I strain to look and listen. It sounds like someone is walking away. We look at each other, curious. Even amid all the activity, Bud and Sis hear us and notice our sudden uneasiness. They sit down beside us and follow our gaze. They look at each other. Dad sees us all gathered together and joins us, looking puzzled.

"Something wrong?" he asks quietly.

"I dunno," Bud says. "We think we saw someone outside and so do the dogs."

Arrorrr, we agree as quietly as we can.

Dad opens the door a crack and peers out. "I don't see a sign of anyone," he says, scratching our ears. "The wind is up, though. Maybe it was just blowing the bushes."

Drool and I know better.

"We need to keep an eye out," Bud whispers to Sis as Dad goes back to the party. "I trust Slobbers' and Drool's instincts."

"Me too," Sis agrees. "Who do you think it could have been?"

"Arrorrr," Drool and I echo together. *Who indeed?*

Lightning Source UK Ltd.
Milton Keynes UK
UKHW021008261120
374135UK00008B/224

9 781636 496719